Life Goes By

LIFE GOES BY

Blake Trombley

iUniverse, Inc.
New York Lincoln Shanghai

Life Goes By

iUniverse, Inc.

For information address:
iUniverse, Inc.
2021 Pine Lake Road, Suite 100
Lincoln, NE 68512
www.iuniverse.com

ISBN: 0-595-33029-0

Printed in the United States of America

Contents

▼

Introduction

Have you ever gone through a routine in your life, just so you could feel alive? Have you ever gone through that one routine which makes you feel whole again? It helps you remember what life is about. Everything in that moment is exactly the same, and all your problems are forgotten. All that matters is getting through the routine. For him, this routine always stayed the same. The details of life never changed.

The city lights would showcase all of New York to an imaginary standpoint. A sparkle of hope would always emerge from an ordinary streetlight. It would blind the eyes for that brief spec of time. It was like he was a deer caught in the head-lights of an oncoming car. The bright pavement road to her apartment was always slippery. The only logical explanation could be the continual bar hopping from drunken fools. Reflections could be seen in water puddles while he was walking the ungracious pavement. He would pause, because it was something he always did. He wasn't reflecting on life. It was like he was there already.

His routine always consisted of a taxi, a bus, a train, and then a momentary walk to an apartment complex he had gone to many times, although this time it took a while, because he wasn't up to speed. He fought hard to get to this point. Even the conditions made it worse. It was cold to a point where his knees felt like frozen Popsicles. His gloves covered his sweaty palms. The weather brought on this horrible pinching sensation to where he couldn't help but wince every two seconds. He wore a pair of baggy blue jeans, which blew back and forth because of the wind. The green turtleneck was faded in color; however, it kept him warm, even though he sacrificed style. He wore a dark black jacket that extended down to his knees, which wasn't very far because he was only 5'9". His once proud black hair was gone.

While exiting the taxi, he placed a baggy red beanie over his head. It didn't take him long to stretch it down past his pointed ears. His white shoes were clean. It was his first new pair in two years. He also got a new pair of glasses. This new pair came extremely thin, to his liking actually. They didn't entirely cover his eyes. At times they would slide down his skinny nose. His beard no longer appeared like it did months ago. He would notice this in the reflection of the gorgeous mirror on the train ride. He could also see what was happening behind him. He watched while a young child played with a Barbie doll. Her parents would participate in the game. It would bring a great smile to his pale and white face.

The walk wasn't needed. A taxi could take him the remainder of the way; however, he insisted on walking because it was something he always did. He always stopped and took an interest in every small store he passed. He would glance inside just to see what kind of display they had. He wouldn't stand around for a long time—the temperature wouldn't let him after falling into the low thirties. He finally made it to the apartment complex. He pressed down the frozen button for the buzzer for as long as the wind blew. After he withdrew, he noticed the icy steps he had just walked up seconds earlier. It actually took longer than seconds because of the struggle at each step. After many nervous steps in one spot, he heard nothing over the receiver. He took two steps back, although he wasn't ready to leave. The door flung open minutes later; meanwhile, someone took off in nursing clothes. In his opinion, he figured she was late for work.

As he entered, the building was cold, sour, and shaky. He didn't remove his jacket even though he passed the smoky heater. The cool air breached the inside with a sharp whistle. It was two grueling flights of stairs to walk. The elevator wasn't working. He piously walked up one step at a time, which led him to the third floor. He leaned against the side of the door while struggling for breath and then knocked three times. He always knocked three times.

He stood by the door, eagerly waiting to tell her something.

"Be right there."

He looked around the hallway; it wasn't very long in distance. The dark hardwood floors didn't provide a gracious welcome. The floors were stained, rotten; therefore, he could only imagine how cold they must have been. The door graciously opened. There she stood, Casey Davis, and she was beautiful even with a robe on. Her body was slender. Her blonde hair fell past her shoulders. Her blue eyes had an impact that made his knees shiver. It wasn't the cold weather anymore. She didn't have any makeup on. She didn't need to. That's the way he loved her. His being there stunned her; therefore, there was a silent lapse while he stood in the doorway.

"Hey," he softly said. His smile vaguely showed. His face was completely tired. He was dreary from the entire ordeal of getting here. He tried to hold it back while he showed a smile. It didn't work.

"What are you doing here?"

"I was sort of looking for a 'hey' in return," he replied. He quietly started to laugh, but hidden, and then he coughed away from the door. He shook his head from side to side as he smiled at her again in the doorway. "You shouldn't be here. Not in your…"

"My condition. I know. I know all about my…condition."

"Carter." She said it so softly and elegantly, yet so coldly. She didn't want him to leave after coming all of this way. However, she didn't want him to spend the time explaining something if he didn't have to.

"Hold on. Just let me say something…ha…well it's funny…you know when you have everything planned out…like what you're going to say at that moment." He took a breath and paused while he nervously pushed down his shirtsleeves. "And now that moment is here and what you wanted to say is gone."

"Carter."

"Just wait…okay…I'm fine. I've lived a life of 'what ifs?'. I've lived it to a point where I can't do it anymore…okay. I've always wanted to say something…to tell you…but…ha…it's always a lot easier in your head…but, I love you. I do. And it's not because of my condition. I've always loved you." He took another deep breath while he carefully coughed. He ran his hand over his beanie after his last cough. She stood there quietly in the doorway while her tears slowly started to fall down her wonderful face.

"And it's funny because I realized it on the way over here…I took the bus, and I walked…and I…didn't know where I was going or why until I actually showed up. Ah…ha…here I am…on your doorstep." He took a step forward but then fell to the ground and he felt the cold hardwood floor. He quietly laughed while she grew concerned. She knelt down to help him during the process of his scared laugh.

"Carter."

"I'm okay."

"Let me help you."

He knelt on one knee while taking dramatic breaths. He stayed there for a short while. She knelt down next to him holding his sweaty right hand. "I'm fine. I don't need help."

"Yes, you do," she replied. She wrapped her right arm around his, and he moved away from his kneeling position but shamelessly fell back down. "Okay. Maybe I do need help."

"No, it's okay…I can manage my way back," he stated while he leaned against the wall of the doorway. He finally got up while clinging to the doorway, to her body in particular. He continued on with his familiar laugh.

"No, you will not. You will stay here, and I'm not letting you go back. I love you too."

"Well, we have great timing, don't we?" he replied as he limped into the room while she carried him the entire way. She joined his laugh, just to feel comfortable while a tear fell from her eye to her cheek. He painlessly moaned and they continued to walk towards the couch. A cat scampered by, jumping on the table faster than Carter's reply.

"Hey, when did you get a cat?"

"I've always had a cat," she replied. He crashed and burned on the couch, then leaned back while she placed a warm blanket around his frozen body. He closed his eyes as she wiped away her tears. "Oh…I guess…I never noticed."

"Just relax okay?" she said as she took off his glasses. She placed them on the table next to the couch.

"I can do that. I'll have a nice dream…about the past…about us…before this," he said. His head rolled down and converged on the small green pillow at the end of the couch. She walked over and adjusted the blanket, kissed his forehead, and then gently kissed his lips. She couldn't help but wipe away another tear from her eye. She turned off the television while walking over towards the telephone. She picked it up and started to dial a number. She punched four numbers. She stopped after looking his way. She hung the phone up nervously. Her silent cry slowly formed as she walked back to the couch. It was all she could do.

CHAPTER 1

▼

FROM THE BEGINNING

"You're told everything, everyone, and anything has a purpose. That's what I was told growing up, and, when you're young you buy into it because it's what you're told, and you don't question it. Then you become older, and you grow wise, and you start to ask questions and judge everything by its appearance. Growing up, it's something that everyone should enjoy, and I did."

—Carter Graham

From the beginning is the place a story usually starts, isn't it? There's a point to starting from the beginning. Everyone knows the point of starting from the beginning because it's the way things go. A story is never told backwards in real life. Therefore, why should it be told backwards now? Why tell a story from the beginning, though, if there isn't a specific interest or memorable ideas? So where do you start? Of course, all of those statements are rhetorical questions. Each of those questions means nothing. What's the meaning of life?

His life always revolved around one place. This one lighthouse off the shores of Long Island came to be his permanent home. He had hopes of leaving at one time. He never did though. It could have been a number of reasons. His reasons matched the number of fishing boats that passed by during fishing season. A boat would pass every five minutes during those months. However, it was a different time of year now. There would be no fishing boats at all during the winter season. Therefore, those reasons for leaving would all consist of empty water.

He watched as the cold ocean water splurged up towards the demented lighthouse. It came, one consisted wave after another. With each wave, the paint from the lighthouse grew tired just like the night sky. The smell of the ocean water wasn't as strong as it normally was. This place was different, different being that it wasn't the ideal place to be in New York. Long Island was beautiful of course; however, this place was something that should have been kept under the radar. For the past month, he could bring out all the negativity of this place. It matched his facial expression every day. It was as if this place brought out the worst in him. It started outside; however, it always had a way of following him inside. He was outside now, although even the smell of outside made him sick. Being inside didn't make him feel much better. After spending time in the moonlight, he headed back inside, knowing what was coming.

He tediously crept back over towards the bathroom, which was considerably bigger than his own room. He knelt over the toilet and stayed there for ten minutes. His treatment was over, although he was still feeling the effects. After gathering himself, he walked gently and cautiously to the top of the lighthouse. His gray pullover sweater hung down to his thighs. He had a red beanie sitting on his head. He pushed it down so it would cover his ears. His bald head became cold after leaving it uncovered for more than an hour. His baggy pants blew back and forth after letting the wind in through the open window. During this time, he drank a cup of hot chocolate. He sipped it in tiny spurts while he sighed each time after sipping. He watched the waves break and the moon hit the water. Its reflection was beautiful. The wind picked up while the whistling grew with intensity in the background. It sounded like a reoccurring song which, given time, would become annoying. Every rock had its place on the shores of Long Island.

"You okay?" His mother asked as she walked into the room. His mother was extremely worried about her son. Although it wasn't because of the problem her son actually had. She had asked this question every ten minutes for the past week. Every time, she would get the same answer.

"I'm fine."

"I think you should see someone. Talk to someone."

He sighed again in frustration. He took another drink from his hot chocolate, but this sip was longer than the usual. He placed the cup down on the table after closing the window. He picked up his cup again and walked over towards his mother. His mother used a cane to walk. It was from an accident four years ago. His mother always had to wear a hat because of it. She always wore a hat inside as well. She wore a circular hat today; however, her son couldn't make out the colors because he didn't have his glasses on. Without them, his sight didn't take to colors or to the words in a book.

He walked by his mother without saying a word. He carefully wandered down the circular steps that led down to the living room. The study was there as well. He spent most of his time in the study. It's where he would read. Reading was something he could never give up. His glasses would be in the study, as usual. When he arrived, he put them on. He noticed his mother's hat. It was pink, of course.

"Who do you want me to talk to?"

"There's a man. His name is Martin. Doctor Martin."

After picking up the book from the table, he flipped through the pages and to the page where he left off. There was a wallet-sized picture used as a bookmark. He used it to mark his pages. It was five wallet-sized pictures in a row that stretched down. He took these pictures in a small booth at a carnival about five months ago. He wasn't alone in the picture either. There was a woman along with him. In four out of the five pictures, they made funny faces. In the last one, he was engaged in a kiss.

"I'm tired of doctors."

"I know, but he's a counselor."

He leaned back against the couch after grabbing a blanket off the end. He covered himself from his waist down. He yawned and then started to read but stopped after a couple of sentences.

"You're not going to leave me alone until I talk to him?"

"I just want you to talk to him. Just once."

"Okay," he replied. He started to read his book again; however, his mother didn't move from her demented spot. He stopped reading. "What?"

"When was the last time you talked to her?"

"Not today, Mom. Okay? Just not today."

He picked up his hardback book again and started to read the second paragraph after his mother walked away. The study room was filled with books. Three of the four walls had elevated bookshelves. Old books occupied almost every shelf. He had probably read half of the books in this room. As of right now, he was reading *A Beautiful Mind*. While reading, his mother started a warm fire for him. The fire sat in the corner of the room. During that time of reading, the heat quickly reached the couch. After ten pages of delightful reading, he became tired. It wasn't long before the heat would put him to sleep.

The night slipped by when finally, after countless hours, sunlight appeared; however, he didn't see it, at least not at first. The study room was blocked from the sun because of peach-colored curtains. The curtains didn't match the color of the room. They never changed the curtains for at least ten years. He took a long time to rise to his feet, although he did notice the book he had been reading from earlier on the floor. He picked it up and placed it down on the end of the couch. The blanket fell to the floor and near his red socks, which now rested at his ankles. He picked up the glasses he left on the table and put them on.

He limped towards the doorway as he always did. However, he stopped by the last bookshelf near the door this time. He continually glanced up at the picture of his father and him. He was thirteen at the time. They both held their fishing poles tight, and their fisherman hats didn't match. His father held up a large fish, which stretched down to his knees, while he held a fish that was no longer than his hand. He grasped the picture with his right hand and stared at it in the doorway. Then he felt the sensation in his hand go. He dropped the picture. The picture cracked against the side of the bookshelf. After five minutes of collecting himself on the floor, he sat up and clenched the picture again.

A tear rolled down his left eye as he wiped it away with his left shoulder. He placed the cracked picture frame back on the bookshelf during his exit. He walked through the living room after noticing all the small reminders his mother kept up so she could always remember her husband. Fishing trophies, stuffed fish, and fishing equipment filled the room, and every blanket on every couch consisted of fish. Even the smell was fish. She never gave up on him. She believed that one day he would return. Carter, on the other hand, gave up a long time ago, although he realized, with his current condition, that he should have kept hope a little longer.

After a late lunch, which consisted of half a muffin, he took a quick four-minute shower. He dressed into the normal apparel for this time of month. He dressed into the same pair of baggy blue jean pants that he wore to bed. He put on a white long sleeved shirt before placing his faded green turtleneck over it. His new white Adidas shoes came out of the box extremely bright, and the laces came at perfect length. After putting them on, he took a couple of steps. He heard the squeaks, which brought comfort to him for some reason. He walked to the door knowing he hadn't bid his mother farewell. It was around two in the afternoon. His mother still wasn't up. He didn't want to wake her because he didn't want to hear the barrage of questioning before he left. He had called a taxi about twenty minutes ago. It was waiting outside now. As soon as he opened the door, the cool air hit him. He knew he needed a jacket. He grabbed the black jacket by the door, which extended down to his knees. He raced the cold breeze while putting it on. He adjusted his beanie while walking out the door of the dingy place he called home.

He walked over towards the taxi while the wind pushed him from side to side. He would watch the water from the corner of his eye. The waves would force themselves upon rocks, one after another, until a break of maybe four seconds would occur. After each wave, the water would go bursting five to ten feet into the air. He loved that sight. He could remember when he was younger; he would go into that water, but only in the summer. The waves would hit his chest with such a dominant force. He would ride them home to his mother's calling. The sun wasn't out today like most days. The dark clouds covered every inch of the sky. There was no rain in the forecast, but, of course, the forecast can always be wrong.

"Where are you headed?" The taxi was surprisingly clean. So was the driver; however, his accent was really strong. He had to repeat what he asked because Carter had trouble hearing him. "Where are you headed?"

"I don't really know the address…but it's about ten miles up the road and to the left…I can point it out when we get there."

"No problem."

The taxi was cold, to say the least. There wasn't a heater going, so it was going to be a very icy ride. During this time, Carter pulled the gloves out of his jacket and put them on rather quickly. He looked out the window while the taxi proceeded down a very narrow road. It was one that brought trouble to those who didn't know it. To both sides, the clear water could be seen, and just watching the cool air come from the water sent shivers to his spine. He could remember a time when he was kid. He fell into the icy lake; it cracked and broke. He must have been about eleven. His father pulled him out that day. He was afraid the entire time, while his father hid his fear for only a certain amount of time. He didn't stop shivering for at least three days.

There wasn't much to look at on the ride to town. He did this ride often, although he never took a taxi anywhere until four months ago. He pulled out the wallet-sized pictures from last night. He couldn't help but glance down at them. It turned to a stare while he took off his right glove. He patiently rubbed his fingers back and forth on each picture. He smiled because of the faces they made. Then he would focus on the last one, which was the color picture. It was their kiss. This was only five months ago. So much changed in just one month. Just knowing that killed him the most.

"Anywhere around here?"

He stopped looking at the pictures. He placed them back in the right pocket of his jacket and then leaned forward. "Right there. To the left." The taxi pulled over in a fire zone, only momentarily though. Carter moved over on his right side while extracting his wallet. He handed the man a twenty. Minutes later, he entered a warm building after taking the elevator up to the third floor. It was only a four-story building' however, he was glad they had an elevator because he wouldn't have walked up three flights of stairs. He exited the elevator on the third floor. It didn't take him long to find the receptionist's desk. There was a man with blonde and curly hair with blue eyes. He looked like one of those sweet boys you only see in movies. He couldn't have been over eighteen years old.

"Can I help you?"

"I'm here for Dr. Martin."

He started to type away on his computer while answering the phone in the same process. He did it so rapidly and quickly that it was finished before Carter could reply.

"Your name?"

"Excuse me, sir. Your name?" he said seconds later.

"Carter Graham."

Carter glanced around the room and noticed that the entire room was empty. It was all covered in new white paint. He found out he was right after his hands became covered in white paint because he accidentally touched the wall. He wiped them off, aggravated at himself.

"Have a seat, and the doctor will be with you shortly."

Carter looked over at the chairs, which were located on the far side of the room. After he managed his strength to get over there, he sat down and gave a long sigh. His name was called right after sitting down. "Dang it. I should have stayed where I was," he whispered as he tenderly shifted his weight forward and got up. The nurse showed him through and led him to the doctor's office. She opened the door while he thankfully walked inside and sat down in the comfortable black chair across from the doctor's desk. The doctor entered the room minutes later. However, during that time of being alone, Carter studied his room.

He noticed a pair of golf trophies on top of the bookshelf. A picture of the doctor with his family was left unattended on his desk. Only the picture occupied the desk. It was placed on the left corner, to Carter's left. He picked up the picture and examined it and smiled because the young boy smiling in the picture reminded him of himself. He had black hair that stretched down and blocked his eyes; his freckles occupied his face, but he would lose them as he grew older. Before he could examine it in more detail, a firm and steady voice came.

"My wife and son."

"It's a nice picture."

The doctor sat down in his chair and placed a notebook, along with his tape recorder. down on his desk. He looked over at Carter, showing only signs of a professional look upon his face. His gray hair was cut short. His beard was gray as well. It wasn't thick at all though. The long sleeves of his blue button-down shirt were rolled up to his forearm. His jacket was placed nicely on his coat rack.

"You keep everything clean."

"I try."

Carter removed his gloves and placed them inside his left jacket pocket. He removed his jacket and placed it on the back of his chair. He looked over at the middle-aged doctor, and his hands were folded over one another on his desk. He was waiting for Carter to say something.

"I've never done this before."

"That's usually the case," the doctor replied.

Carter coughed. He grew irritated at his own cough after a certain amount of time. He noticed the large bookshelf on the left side of the room. It was covered with books. Everything had its place, just like a rock on the shores of Long Island. It was beautiful to Carter.

"You know…life can be summed up right now with that bookshelf and those books. I mean, you look at them, and everything has its place, right then and there, but yet…" Carter rose from his chair and walked over to the bookshelf. His head rolled up and down many times while the doctor watched in curiosity.

"Yet there's always a book or books out of place…sort of like life. There's the ones you know by heart…the ones you're familiar with…the ones you hate, love…and then there's…" He stopped after pulling a book from the shelf. It was a cookbook from the medicine section. He showed it to the doctor and smiled. "I bet you don't know how that got there," Carter said as he placed the cookbook in the right section.

"I don't."

Carter walked back over to the chair and sat down. He took another sigh, after coughing forcefully three times. "So you're comparing your life to a bookshelf, and you're the book that's been shelved out of place?"

"No," Carter replied.

"Then what are you?"

Carter took a deep breath. His light brown eyes engaged towards the bookshelf and he smiled. He brought his focus back to the doctor, still showing his same smile. "I'm the book that hasn't been read. No one knows the story, or the ending, or even the reason behind it, because no one has ever read it."

"When did you find out you had…"

"Cancer…about four months ago. It's what you were going to ask, wasn't it?" He took his frustrated coughs with consistency as always after replying. "And when you found out…" the doctor started, but Carter interrupted as he vigorously moved from his chair again. He was engaged upon the bookshelf.

"You've never read these books before, have you?"

Carter pointed to the left side of the bookshelf. It was at the top row at the very far end next to the window. Carter ran his fingers over the books. His pale fingers rubbed them one by one until he heard an answer from the doctor.

"No, I haven't."

"Why not?"

Carter removed a book from the bookshelf. He showed the doctor before he could answer. Carter opened the brand new book. It was the first time the book had ever been opened. It wasn't creased at all. It was brought to life for that split second.

"I just never got around to it, I suppose."

"It's funny how people say that…yet they keep them on their shelves."

Carter flipped through the book and then placed it back where it belonged on the shelf. He gently walked back to his seat yet again. He continued to look over at the doctor with his same smile. The doctor worked up another question.

"What are you doing?"

"I'm waiting for you to ask me a question," Carter replied.

"Any question?"

Carter shook his head "no" four times while he gradually smiled. "It has to be the right question, the perfect question," he replied. He shifted his eyes over at the bookshelf again, trying to give the doctor a hint.

"You want to talk about what's on the bookshelf?"

Carter once again smiled after shaking his head "no." "Not that particular bookshelf. What's the best way to find a book you've never heard of or read?"

"You want to talk about your bookshelf?"

"Exactly," Carter replied as he pointed at the doctor with his smile again. Carter noticed the bookshelf again and walked towards it. The golf trophies caught his attention this time. They sat on top of the four-shelf bookshelf.

"What, exactly, is on your bookshelf?"

"Not much," Carter replied. "Why do you keep these trophies?"

The doctor pulled his head up in high achievement as he looked at the trophies. He smirked and said, "I take pride in what I won."

"Really. So these trophies kind of tell the stories themselves."

"You want to hear the story?" the doctor asked.

"No…it's like skipping to the end of the book. I see the trophy. You won."

Carter walked back to his seat. Finally he sat down for the final time. He adjusted his beanie after rolling up his turtleneck sleeves to his forearm. They quickly fell back down to his wrists. He didn't try again.

"You asked me what's on my bookshelf? It's not much, but it's difficult."

"Well, start from the beginning." The doctor adjusted his shirt, twice.

Carter continued to smile. "I can't really start from the beginning. How about four months ago?…when…all this happened."

"Okay," the doctor replied. He hit the record button on his tape recorder; however, Carter noticeably moved towards the desk. He turned it off after bringing it to his side of the table. He placed it on the floor. The doctor gazed at him the entire time. "You don't want me to record it?"

"There are certain stories or books that should only be heard or read once." Carter kept his smile while the doctor nodded along.

He waited for Carter to begin; however, Carter took his time to get ready. Carter sighed, a sigh that was no different than the usual one. He closed his eyes for no more than four breaths. He nervously laughed again. Then he stopped laughing and brought his attention over to the doctor after composing himself.

"You're told everything, everyone, and anything has a purpose. That's what I was told growing up, and, when you're young, you buy into it because it's what you're told, and you don't question it. Then you become older, and you grow wise, and you start to ask questions and judge everything by its appearance. Growing up, it's something that everyone should enjoy, and I did."

"And then?" the doctor replied.

Carter took another breath while he tearfully took off his red beanie. His bald head showed as he sadly rubbed it twice. He held back his tears. "And then…something happens…Life happens…ha…you learn something new every day, don't you?"

CHAPTER 2

▼

CLASSIC

"A lie can travel halfway around the world while the truth is putting on its shoes."

—Mark Twain

It was the month of June, Friday, the eleventh. It was a time when everything seemed perfect in the world. The sun magically appeared after storm clouds disappeared. A cool breeze came from the shore on a day of life at its finest moment. The wind rustled against his pants while his smile matched the intensity of the breeze. He held her hand while they walked the temperate shore. He finally stopped complaining about the bottom of his khaki pants because they were covered in water from walking through the water. It was her idea, and she would continue to make small splashes just to annoy him.

It was the summer. The salty water smelled as fresh as an open can of tuna. The lighthouse was in the distance; it looked completely different from afar. Up close, it was dirty, old, and it had a consistent smell of old life. Its rusted stairs would take away all prestige that was shown from a distance. From this perspective, five hundred yards away, the view was extraordinary. The lighthouse looked in perfect condition from that sandy spot that some call home. It was young again.

His pants were soaked in water up to his knees. His shirt was left untouched. He wore a white T-shirt now, although he did have on a nice shirt earlier. The shirt from earlier was covered in spaghetti; it was her fault. He hated spaghetti, but she made it anyway. About halfway into making it, they spilled sauce on their clothes, well, on his clothes, his elegant light blue shirt, and she could only laugh at him while he stood there with his legs spread out and his hands held in the air. He retaliated by throwing spaghetti in her hair; however, she fearlessly pressed it against his face. She smothered him with it, all the way down his neck. The pasta fell to the floor. The romantic lunch that was planned no longer existed, although the romance did. He engaged in a tiny kiss. Then she swooped in and they kissed for what almost seemed like minutes. His entire body was covered in tasteless sauce. After minutes of trying to clear it off with a towel, they decided to take a walk, to walk the surreal shores.

They both cleared the sauce from their faces. He ran his hair through the water after spitting out the nasty sauce. His short black hair still was marked by a couple of stains; however, she picked them away. He removed fragments of sauce from her hair. He couldn't help but give her a kiss each time. It was a speck of a kiss after each fragment. She had blue eyes that matched the color of the ocean water, and that ocean water was so clear that you could see the sand when walking out just before the wave hit you. Her blonde hair reminded him of dandelions. Even when he ran his fingers through her hair, it consisted of softness.

It was only two in the afternoon on a cool summer day. She departed and went home to her apartment complex, which was across town while he approached his own home. Birds flew by, making their annoying sound that he grew to love. His smile diminished down to a weak frown. He waited patiently as he watched the minutes go by on his watch. He had done this growing up; however, this was the first time he did this in years. He knew that it was hopeless. He did it as a kid, waiting endlessly, impatiently, for his father to return from a fishing trip.

"Why did you wait for your father that day?"

Carter reluctantly changed his smirk to a puzzled stare. He positioned his chair towards the bookshelf again. "Why does someone wait? I don't know...I can only imagine that...that day, something different would have happened. It brought me back to childhood for that moment."

Carter exited his chair. This time he used the desk to guide him back to the bookshelf. He pulled a book from the bookshelf; the farthest shelf to be exact, next to the window. He looked the book over front and back before opening it.

He couldn't help but run through each page. He stopped after sorting through about ten pages.

"Do you know what this book is about?"

"No. That's from the section I never read," the doctor replied. He took a sip from his rich cup of coffee, which his young receptionist brought in moments ago.

"It's about a man who falls in love...with a woman, and she has an illness...and he doesn't figure it out until he's in love. Or how about this one? Have you read this one? It's funny...how all these books are so similar...yet so apart."

"What happened after you waited that day?"

"My mother, and then...the carnival."

Carter turned around and walked back to his comfortable chair. He shifted his weight back against the soft part of the chair. "The carnival...that's a day I will always remember. No one can take that away from me. It's great...but then there was one part...one part from that night that I wish I could change."

His mother entered the room while he put on a pair of light blue jeans. They weren't as baggy as his usual style. Casey bought these for him. He didn't want to tell her that she got the wrong size. He watched his mother while looking at himself in the mirror. She wore a white hat no bigger than her pear-shaped head. It was a very squinty hat. Her hair extended down to her skinny waist. She was a brunette, although she did have strands of blonde in her hair, which came from the terrible dye she had used weeks ago. Her green eyes reflected in the mirror, and Carter turned around while putting on his raggedy Adidas shoes, which weren't white anymore because dirt made an imprint on every inch of his shoes. He wore a white shirt, which consisted of a local brand name imprinted on the left side. His body was extremely fit. He worked out on a regular basis. His boxing bag rested in the closet in the hallway; he would bring it out once a day and do the usual boxing routine. It consisted of push-ups, pull-ups, and then shower. A blue bag rested in the corner of the hallway where college books spilled out one by one.

His mother's face was very pale today. She never left the house, so that would be the reason, although she still wore a hat inside. There was a reason for it, of course; however, it wasn't a very good reason to Carter. It wasn't a reason that should be shared, at least not right away. Her face was flat like the actresses who starve themselves. Her nose didn't point out like Carter's did, and her ears were curved. Carter had his father's look. He received nothing from his mother except her hair, which is why he hated his hair. It was flat just like his mother's face.

"Going out?" his mother asked.

"What does it looks like?" Carter kicked the bag of books over. They all consisted of English literature. He walked into the bathroom where he washed his face. He trimmed his beard and goatee as well; it was all the process of approval.

His mother glanced down at the bag of books while she entered the sober bathroom. She asked, "Only a year left?"

"What does it looks like?"

He exited the bathroom while putting on a hat with a Long Island fishing scene on it. It even had a stick figure holding a pole waiting for a fish to bite. "I still can't believe you wear that hat."

"It fits me."

"I remember your father gave it to you."

Carter grew disgruntled and walked out of the room while shutting his light off in the process. He left his past ridden mother standing alone in the doorway. "I'm just surprised you haven't taken it from my room and placed it in the living room yet," Carter said as he turned off the bathroom light.

"Why would I do that?"

"It's what you always do."

Carter grabbed his wallet, which lay at the end of the hallway on a small coffee table. He had about three hundred dollars in his wallet, in cash. That would be the last paycheck he would get for a while. He quit his job two days ago, from the fishing boat. He did it because he didn't want to go out to sea anymore, to become his father, although he still wore the same clothes that his father did when he went fishing.

"Why did you quit your job?" the doctor interrupted and asked.

"I didn't want to become my father," Carter replied as he adjusted his chair. He rubbed his hand over his head while grimacing before taking a sip of water from the glass on the desk, which lay next to the doctor's family picture. Such a wonderful family it was. It was one of those pictures you see inside a picture frame at a store.

"How come you didn't want to become your father?"

"Can I tell the story?" Carter sarcastically implied while smiling.

The doctor smirked along with him. "Sorry, I'm new at this."

"That's usually the case," Carter replied, hinting at the doctor's comment from earlier. They shared a short laugh before Carter reluctantly continued.

His mother left the doorway after closing the door behind her. She had a knack for closing every door that was open. She did it to a point that it had to be done right away, after someone just used it. Minutes later, Carter would go back into the bathroom, turn on the light, brush his teeth, and then turn the light off again. His mother would once again close the door while Carter proceeded down the hall. The time was almost seven while the chimes on the clock made their tremendous noise. His mother would smile when hearing the chimes. It brought back the grace of old life. She would grab her cane before walking into the living room. She would stare at the entire collage of fishing reminders while the chimes died.

His mother would spin in circles in that room, literally. Carter watched in disapproval. He could only shake his head, indicating her stupidity. Every night at seven in the evening, it was her routine. Carter knew it by heart. She danced for two minutes. Then she started a thing of tea, while she sang the same song over and over. It was her wedding song. She would sing it horribly out of tune, like drunken orderlies do to a jukebox. She would bring the glass of tea back into the living room where she would sit on the couch and stare out into nothing, while consistently drinking her tea. For some reason, Carter watched every time. Every time, he hoped his mother would do something different. She never did.

"He's not coming back, Mom."

She would ignore him.

He would walk past her; however, she would break her moment and ask, "Where are you going?"

Carter would turn around and smirk because this was something he had dealt with for four years now. He would face his mother while she had this confused look on her face. He wouldn't look at her for more than seconds; therefore, he walked away saying, always saying, "I'll be back later."

Carter left the house. He took the only car they had, which was a sedan. It consisted of multiple dents; however, it ran fine. He headed to town, which would be a brisk drive. When he arrived, he was welcomed by Casey. She wore a very classy outfit. It wasn't anything special; however, she made it look fantastic. It was a pair of tight blue jeans with a rosy red shirt. The sleeves stopped at her elbows. Carter found it hard just to say "Hi".

Carter took his normal breaths after sighing. He coughed like a bee humming for honey. He looked over at the window, which rested just above the bookshelf. The window didn't show the outside world.

"So that was the night of the carnival?"

"Best night of my life."

Carter hesitantly moved forward while he rested his elbows on his knees. He took courageous breaths after struggling with the taste of tap water. He wiped the water away from his mouth with his right sleeve. "It was the best night of my life, but even…the best nights…have their moments of regret."

"Was your mother the regret part?"

"Ha…no…it should be, it should have been…but it's not. My mother had her problems, and after a while I grew tired…tired where I wanted her to understand he wasn't going to come back…but she could never understand."

"What happened to your mother?" the doctor asked.

Carter crept out of his chair before walking to the right side of the room where a file cabinet sat. It had three incredibly clean drawers from top to bottom. His eyes focused as he looked it up and down. He grasped the top drawer. He was going to open it; however, he asked for the doctor's permission first.

"You don't mind if I…?"

"Go ahead."

Carter opened the drawer. Of course, it was empty. He laughed after opening each one. After his last laugh, he closed the bottom drawer with his foot. He gingerly walked back to his chair and sat down again. He stared at the doctor with his implanted look of curiosity.

"Why have a cabinet if it's empty?"

"I don't know. Maybe I'm looking to put something there in the future," the doctor replied.

Carter smirked again. It was as consistent as the wind on a rainy night on the beach. Carter kept his attention on the desk as he fixated his eyes on the picture in general.

"Why is this entire room empty? How long have you been here?"

"Six months. I don't know why it's empty. I like it this way."

Carter looked the doctor up and down repeatedly while the doctor caught onto his catchy laugh. Carter felt the desk from end to end before grabbing the picture again for a split second. After that split second, he placed it back down and looked at the desk.

"My mother should have done this."

"Done what?"

"This right here," Carter replied. He walked over towards the trash can next to the right of the desk, picked up a piece of crumbled paper, and placed it in the trash can. The doctor watched him the entire time while he waited for Carter to say something else. He didn't. He returned to his chair just watching the doctor, while the doctor moved his notebook to the other corner of his desk. After moving the useless notebook to the corner of the desk, he folded his arms over again.

"Done what?" the doctor asked again. He was interested in hearing Carter's answer. Carter knew this because the doctor no longer leaned back in his chair.

"She should have done this right here." Carter turned his chair towards the miraculous bookshelf. He swung his chair without any hesitation towards the empty cabinet. He carefully brought it back towards the dismal desk. "She should have done this. Cleared out memories of the past."

She held his hand tight, as they raced from one ride to the next. They had to run because of a local officer. The officer caught them kissing on one of the rides. He was just trying to run them down so he could have a nice chat with them; however, they couldn't be caught. She brought him over to one of the basketball games at the carnival after ditching the officer.

"Win me a stuffed animal," she said as she finally let go of Carter's right hand. He was actually impressed by the entourage of stuffed animals.

"Why? You want to run it over with your car like you did last time?" He started to laugh; however, she didn't hesitate to respond.

"That was an accident."

"I hope you don't do that to me."

She wrapped her arms around his neck while she pressed her firm body in against his. She took comfort in his arms for minutes as he stumbled back because he tried to walk forward during the duration of her holding him. He stepped into a small hole in the dirt, which ultimately led to his stumble.

"Please," she insinuated over and over.

"Okay. Okay."

Carter placed down a crisp ten-dollar bill on the table. He was given five basketballs, crappy rubber ones. His shot was horrendous. The first two he air balled; he could only scratch his head in astonishment. He hit nothing but backboard on the third try after scratching his head for good luck; it was his way of playing off his air balls.

"You suck."

"Thanks for the vote of confidence," Carter replied as he shot the fourth ball. It wasn't even close. "They make these rims entirely too small."

"I don't know what you're complaining about. You haven't even touched the rim," Casey replied. He shot the last ball; however, he missed on purpose. Surprisingly, it was closer than all of the other shots.

"Next time," he said as he placed his arm around her. They joyfully walked away from the unviable table. They did the cotton candy; however, they got rid of it bites later. They continued to ride the rides; however, during every ride, the same officer would catch them. They would have to run again while Carter would grew tired of it; however, Casey would drag him along, when he would finally get caught up in the hunt with her.

Minutes later. the officer was off their scent. Carter brought her back towards the impossible game section. He walked down the long row of crazy games. He stopped at the very end where the football game presented itself. You would throw the ball through a circular hole and if you made three out of five, you would win a prize.

He placed down ten bucks while he was given five perfect footballs. He rested them on the counter in front of him while he looked at Casey. "Which one do you want?"

"Oh, you think you can do it, son?" the old man behind the counter asked. His hat was tipped forward and his smile wasn't sincere. He was trying to bait him to play for more money.

"I'll hit five out of five."

Carter adjusted his hat while picking up one of the perfect footballs. Casey stood back while Carter moved his arm in a circular motion to warm up. During this time, his cocky smile grew.

"Tell you what. If you get five out of five, you can pick any of these prizes you want. Throw when ready."

Carter circled his neck after looking over at Casey's embarrassed face. Her sarcastic smile showed, as well as his charismatic smile. He threw the first ball and it went straight through the narrow hole. So did the next. He couldn't miss on any. There was only one ball left while the old man's mouth was wide open, almost bigger than the circular target. He was considerably shocked.

"Why don't you give me a moving target? Make it a bit harder for me," Carter expressed while he circled his arms. He had a crowd of family spectators watching. The old man pushed the circle, and it rocked back and forth. He stood back and watched Carter warm up while Carter continued on with his usual routine. It didn't change. Casey turned her head away while her face became red. It matched her shirt. Of course, he did it without any problem. Casey was allowed to pick a prize.

"Where did you play?"

"I didn't." Carter replied. He smiled again after patting the old man on the back as he walked away with Casey. She picked out a humongous blue beaver. She placed it in Carter's hand; however, he had to hold it with both hands. She wrapped her arms around his clenched waist. The night was still young, and so was he. It was his birthday today; he was twenty-two years old.

"I love you. You know that," she said. He stopped dead in his tracks, while she continued on for three steps. She walked back to him. He didn't say anything at all.

"Hey, I want to marry you," she playfully expressed. His dimwitted smile left while his face was motionless. He hesitantly laughed while looking away because he couldn't look into her eyes for that moment. She stood there waiting for him to say something.

"Hey! You two," the officer from earlier noticed them. Once again Casey grabbed him by the hand as they ran with the blue beaver, although minutes later Carter was trapped inside the house of mirrors. The officer followed them inside.

Carter lost Casey on one of the turns, although they reunited turns later; however, during the duration of his turns, Carter ran into a mirror. Casey would laugh at him; it was her laugh that gave them away. Carter was trapped while the officer forcefully walked towards them. They both knelt against the mirror, with the beaver protecting them. "Now you two..." the officer started. He was quickly interrupted by both Carter and Casey.

"Hey, Mr. Davis."

"Hi, Dad."

Carter coughed while leaning forward in his wonderful chair. He took another dreadful sip of water. The doctor wrote some notes earlier on his notebook; however, it was back in its position again, left untouched. Carter was beginning to think that the notebook had nothing to do with him. The room became dark as Carter's eyes became dreary, although he managed not to show any signs. To the doctor's displeasure, he didn't know. "Why didn't you tell her?"

"Ah...ha...that I loved her. I don't know."

"Do you?"

Carter took another humiliating sip of water. He placed the empty glass down on the table while he ran his fingers over the stained glass. He leaned back against his chair yet again. He looked behind the doctor's desk and noticed a dying plant in need of life. It was only about three feet tall. "Can I have another glass of water?" The doctor pressed down his intercom button and asked the young man for another glass of water.

"I do love her. I didn't say it because...I was afraid."

"Afraid of what?"

After the long tremulous talk with Casey's father, they went on two more rides; however, they left early, ducked out. They went back to the lighthouse where they would set up a small blanket so they could relax on the shore. Every now and then, boats would go by like tomorrow's mail. The waves would barely reach the rocks, like Carter barely reached the stars. Casey would shift her weight; therefore, her head rested on his chest. They both gazed up at the night sky like innocent squirrels. The stars weren't as noticeable on normal nights. The light-house blocked the view during every change in conversation.

They both went to different schools; however, since they were only twenty miles apart; he would go to her apartment on a routine basis at night. She would come to his lighthouse, like tonight. They would sit and relax for hours on the hill.

"Where do you think we'll be ten years from now?" she asked.

"Where do you want to be?"

He always stalled on questions like these because he didn't know how to answer them, much less like when people asked them. Casey usually did. After a while, he grew into hearing them. The light passed by again and it blinded Carter's eyes for more than the usual second. He lost sensation in his leg for a moment. He couldn't hear anything. He knew Casey was talking; however, he couldn't say anything. Then the awkward moment was gone. What happened?

"Carter, did you hear me?"

"Sorry, what was it?"

The light passed again. The same sensation did not occur as before. He started to swallow while making huge gulps. He took hard breaths while holding his head up. He dropped his head back down though so Casey wouldn't ask a question. He wouldn't know how to answer it.

"No matter where we end up, it will be great," she repeated a second time. "Do you agree?"

Carter leaned forward in his chair again so he could grab the new glass of water that sat on the desk. He smelled it before taking a small sip. He rose to his feet again and walked around the room carrying the glass of water in his hand. He paced back and forth nervously.

"That's when it first started?"

"Yeah…but I didn't know…I just didn't…know."

The doctor was going to say something else; however, Carter interrupted him yet again. He walked over behind his desk towards the nearly dead plant. He studied it from all angles while the doctor moved his chair around so he could face the plant. Carter gently positioned the water glass over the leaves and stems and very carefully let the water drip down.

"This needs water. You know that, right? If you don't do it…it loses, it dies. Of course, you know that?"

"I do."

Carter continued to do what he was doing as he moved the glass of water around the entire plant until the water glass was empty. He placed the glass back on the shiny, well cared for table. He rubbed a leaf of the plant a couple of times with his right index finger and thumb. The leaf was brown, definitely in need of plucking.

"Why don't you do it?"

"Just don't have the time…that sounded like a cliché."

"It did," Carter replied. He retracted the leaf off the plant while he looked it over before tossing it into the trash can by the desk. He looked the plant over again and did the same with another leaf, and another.

"It's always about time…time…time…time. Sorry, but I hate time. You can water the plant. Give it its treatment and make sure it's healthy, and it can live a few more months, or you can leave it alone, and let it die…a tired and lonely death. Kind of sounds…familiar, doesn't it?…sorry, I'm a bit of a dramatic."

"It doesn't have to be that way."

Carter walked back towards his rich chair. He sat down again while kicking his feet up for a while. A moment of silence fell and during that duration Carter's eyes closed. The doctor grew concerned. Carter reopened his eyes a question later.

"You okay?"

"Yeah…I'm fine. Where was I?"

Their laughter grew as he walked her to her apartment door, and they stood in the doorway, for days it seemed, holding each other, laughing, and kissing each other. On normal nights, he would go inside and spend the night with her, but her father was in town this weekend; therefore, he would go home.

"I'll see you tomorrow, right?" she asked.

"Of course."

Carter kissed her again while she opened the door. He almost fell in the process as she laughed again. They engaged in yet another kiss. He leaned against the door while she continued to kiss him; however, they stopped because she heard her father's voice down the hall. Carter laughed as he took a step out of the doorway while her father walked through.

"I'll see you tomorrow," Carter expressed. He kissed her elliptical lips once again, even with her father grunting in the background. She closed the door while Carter walked down the hallway. Her father looked her over with his stern look, although it didn't last long. He perked a smile. "I love him," she whispered while her father's smile stretched from wall to wall.

Carter pressed down the button for the elevator. Once again he felt the sensation go as he fell against the side of the elevator, grasping for breath. He fell to one knee. He couldn't move. After ten seconds of kneeling there, he got the sensation back. He effortlessly rose up; however, he was worried. He went home, and, when he arrived, his mother was still listening to the same song. She put a dent in the record player with this song alone.

He entered the room where his mother stood. At this point, his vision became blurry, even with his glasses on. He took them off and cleaned them, but he still had the same problem. He shifted from side to side while almost collapsing on the unsteady table. He tried to remain stable but couldn't. His mother didn't break from her listening or her dancing. She did notice that her son was acting different, but she thought he was joining her party.

"You okay, honey? You want me to get your father?"

Carter wanted to shout at his mother to get over it. He couldn't. He fell to one knee while his mother grew concerned. The music still played on, and the end was coming. Carter fell to the ground grasping for air. He couldn't move. His mother ran over to him and knelt to help him. She didn't know what to do. The music stopped as the record player started to scratch the record. Carter thought it was over just like that song. His mother cried and could only think of one thing to do. "FRANK! FRANK! HELP ME, PLEASE, FRANK."

The next time Carter awoke he was in the hospital with Casey at his side. He leaned over to his side. He noticed doctors talking; conversations lingered in the background although he couldn't make out the words. He didn't stay awake long. He went to sleep again while drowning out the situation.

"It's funny…it happened that quickly," Carter said as he took his normal coughs.

"Who's Frank?"

"My father. My mother had this obsession that he was still there. She needed to clear her past, and she didn't. She…held on to it. It's actually amazing…that I made it to the hospital, ha…I might have been there all night, knowing my mother."

Carter closed his eyes again while the doctor watched as Carter's smile appeared.

"You hungry?" the doctor asked.

"No, thank you."

"So you decided to go through with the treatment?"

"Actually no…not at first, but Casey…convinced me to. I didn't see the point, anymore. My mother, on the other hand, was trying to force me to do it…and she kept…haha…saying my father would make me…when we got back home."

"How come you didn't see the point to it?"

Carter parted ways with his chair again and walked around the room a bit. He had to get up so he didn't lose sensation in his legs. That was his rule, not the doctors. He looked at the empty room before glancing back at the doctor again.

"So when are you going to put belongings in your office?"

"I like it the way it is. So I suppose…never."

"Uh…empty, okay," Carter replied as he walked back to his seat again. He had made a permanent mark in his chair by now. He didn't need to adjust while sitting down anymore. "I didn't see the point because it would only give me a few extra months. What does that give you?"

He knelt over the dramatic, sappy toilet. He had been there for hours. After radiation treatment, his entire face and body were different, fragile. His hair was gone; so was his beard. He cried for hours while kneeling over the toilet. He wanted to be left alone. Even now, his mother would still do her usual routine; however, this time Casey was around to witness it. She didn't tell Carter anything about it; she knew better. After a while, Carter managed his way into the living room, and he had to watch his mother do her same old rainy routine.

She did it even though it was so annoying to everyone. Carter grew irritated by everything his mother did. He had to say something. His mother walked by and gave him a kiss. She was so dreadfully cheerful. Carter reached for her hat as she went by; however, he missed. The next time around, Carter grabbed the hat from her head. She gasped as if she saw the devil.

"Shut off the music. Casey…shut off the music, please," Carter said as he held the hat away from his mother as she tried to grab it from him. He dropped it to the floor after his mother accidentally bumped him in the gut. The music stopped as Carter moaned in pain. He waved for his mother to get away. She grabbed her hat and walked away, although she tried to give her son a kiss before going. Carter refrained as hard as he could. He tried to push her away. He didn't do a very good job of it; however, his yell was harder than a push.

"Damn it, Mom! Give it a rest." He grabbed her hat again and flung it across the room with all his strength. He collected his newfound breath. His mother stood there again, and this time she was saddened by what her son had done. "He's not coming back for you. When are you going to realize that?" His mother started to smile. He knew she was going to say something; therefore, he interrupted before his insane mother could actually say some stupid comment about her once great husband.

"He's gone, okay. What the hell is wrong with you?"

"Carter," Casey exclaimed.

"She needs to know this. I can't deal with this day in and day out…not anymore." Carter got off the couch. He pushed his mother aside but fell to the floor a few steps later. He became angry as he pounded the hardwood floor.

"Damn it!" Casey ran to his aid as he tried to get up. He moved his arm away in a demeaning manner whenever she tried to help him. "I can do it." He left the room but fell again when he reached the bathroom. He hit his elbow on the bathroom counter. Casey came running again while he yelled in pain. She held him while he leaned on her shoulder, and he wept, wept like a baby.

He cried the night away. He didn't move from that spot for hours. Casey would go make something, soup, for instance; however, he wouldn't eat it. Even if he did eat it, he couldn't keep it down. He stayed by that toilet all night while Casey would visit him, although most of the time he wanted to be left alone. His mother would continue to do her usual spiritual routine. Carter would keep crying, no matter how long that record played.

"Your mother didn't understand you?"

"I think she did…but she didn't want to believe it…a nd you can't really…you know…change, unless you actually believe in what you're changing to."

"Were you really angry?"

Carter sighed and laughed, sighed first, and then laughed. He ran his hand over his face while squeezing it like they do in drama television shows. After that, he brought his hand back down to his thigh, where his fingers would tap his pant leg every two seconds. He wasn't thinking about what to say. He knew what he wanted to say. He figured it's always good to think something before you actually say it.

"I may have been angry at God…and I didn't know why…I mean, I guess you could say that my condition played into it, but I was never a big believer in the beginning. I guess…ha…well, I hated Him for the family given to me, which I shouldn't have. You know your father…he's gone…and then your mother, who is totally insane at times, and then there's me…who is actually normal…well, what is normal? Then you're hit, like its nothing, and you're actually scared for the first time in your life…like really scared. So you could ask the why questions…but where would it get you? It will get you back where you started…because nothing has changed since asking. So was I angry?…no…I was just using it as a excuse to express a few things that should have been said a long time ago."

A month went by. Nothing changed; well some things changed; however, the situation remained the same. Cherno was over, as well as radiation therapy. He still felt the effects of plastered medication being thrown into his body. As of right now, he sat on a warm couch with Casey. She placed a blanket over their legs while she put on the television show "Friends." She laughed and giggled every time a joke appeared. That was every breath for her.

He wasn't really an avid "Friends" watcher, although he watched it because she loved the show. She would giggle away every five minutes as if she were a rooster crowing for the sun. The only time Carter would laugh, and it would be a low laugh, was when Chandler said something sarcastic.

"Why are you here?" Carter asked during a commercial break. The usual commercial silence was killing him. "Why am I here?"

"Yeah, why are you here? I don't get it...I mean, I get it, but there's no future...here. I mean..."

"Don't say that. We'll be fine. You will hear the results next week, and everything will be fine. I'm here because I love you. You know that."

Carter's eyes stayed closed while the room became pitch black to him. His eyes were extremely dry, and the doctor handed him another glass of water. "Can I be excused for a little bit? I'll be right back," Carter stated. He didn't wait for an answer. He was already headed towards the door. The doctor opened it for him while showing him the restroom. It looked as if the doctor was going to go in with him. Carter quickly spoke. "I'm not that bad...ha, okay?"

Carter looked at himself in the mirror while turning on the cold water. He let it run while he ran his fingers through the water. He closed his eyes again as he stood there, while the water ran. It slowly drizzled down the drain.

"Do you remember where we first met?" she asked, while she rolled over in the incredibly soft bed. She faced him while they lay underneath the silk covers with their bare bodies shivering from the coldness of the room. Her bedroom was quietly softened by the glow of the dark stars planted on her ceiling. Therefore, he could see the smile on her face. He would kiss her forehead after running his fingers gently across her soft lips. He moved closer to her while her hair fell on top of his head.

"I played against you in an intramural game for college. I filled in for a friend, and you were impressed with my quarterbacking skills. I just had to wiggle a couple of times and I had you burned."

"That's not true," she replied with a hysterical laugh as she playfully slapped his wrist. "Oh yeah, I believe one play you actually stayed in one spot and watched me. You didn't even move from the line of scrimmage."

"Now you're just full of yourself," she said. She had her same laugh as she tried to slap his wrist again; however, he caught it while laughing along with her.

They rolled over on the bed and almost fell off. Their laughter stopped. He kissed her as they rolled back to the center of the bed.

The water was piling up in the sink. He noticed it; therefore, he pulled the plug from the drain. He washed his face before turning off the water. He watched it circulate down, sort of like his life. He wiped his hands before heading back towards the room. After relaxing in his chair for five minutes, he looked around the room, but the doctor wasn't anywhere to be found. He closed his eyes while he rested his head on the back of the chair. He didn't budge from his place of relaxation.

"We had a great time, didn't we?"

"Oh yeah. I always love the opera," he sarcastically implied.

Her red dress fell to her ankles. It was a low cut dress that was specially made for her, a beautiful woman. As for him, he wore a suit, which was an original black and white tuxedo. He did wear a blue vest with a blue tie underneath. He looked very sharp. He even had the pocket watch that went along with it. He opened up the watch while keeping his sarcastic tone; "It is now eight at night."

"You enjoyed it. You know you did."

"I did. I admit it. I always love watching people yell and sing at the top of their lungs…ha, no, actually I loved seeing you in this dress."

It was time to take a taxi home, although he had a different idea. He whistled for a carriage to come over, only in New York. He paid the driver after asking for a special request. He helped her in while he handed her a rose, which he kept hidden from her most of the night. She smiled, and he gave her a kiss. They both sat down on the red leather seats.

"Where to?" the driver asked.

"Anywhere she wants to go."

"Do you know where the art museum is?" she asked.

The driver nodded his head. "You know this way is going to take forever," Carter implied as he smiled without hesitation. She replied, "I know." She moved over to him and engaged in another kiss of love.

The door slammed shut, and Carter opened his eyes. His attention shifted over towards the doctor while he walked over to his chair and sat down.

"Are you tired? We don't have to do this all in one session if you don't want to."

"I'm okay."

Carter looked at the cheap ten-dollar clock before bringing his attention back to the doctor. Carter continued to look around the room, like he did when he first arrived. The doctor would watch him every time his eyes shifted.

"You're waiting for me to ask the right question again?"

"Indeed, I am," Carter replied. He grinned after shutting his eyes again. He closed them in such relaxation; it was like he had a visual image appear before his unopened eyes. He waited for a question, the question that would break his visual image. It would reopen his eyes. Sure enough, it was the right question.

"What happened to your mother?"

CHAPTER 3

▼

WISH IT WERE A DREAM

"Neither a lofty degree of intelligence nor imagination nor both together go to the making of genius. Love, love, love, that is the soul of genius."

—Mozart

August opened up unlimited numbers of options, mostly worries. August was a time where circumstances looked better; however, in actuality, they weren't. Although looks are deceiving, it was a rainy night, and the lightning and thunder rose to a strong roar. The sound soared over sirens in the background every two seconds. The lights flickered while the television shut off; however, seconds later they came back on again. The couch occupied the middle of the empty living room, which was surrounded by white walls as well as white carpet. There were three stains of red wine on the floor. Each was hidden by something specific. The coat rack was next to the door, which was brown and long. Two hangers held on for dear life. The small coffee table in front of the couch covered the other two stains.

The kitchen might have been as big as his room, although it was substantially cleaner. Everything was set in place, like a normal housewife would have done it. Gloves were turned inside out and placed neatly next to the sink. A small pink towel covered the dishes, which were washed an hour ago.

The bedroom was huge by his standards. The great landscape of a bed covered most of it. It was the biggest bed he had ever slept in. He wasn't sleeping now. He was resting with his feet off the bed. His feet dangled like strings from a puppet. Country music breached the background. It wasn't loud; however, it could be heard if someone listened for it. He finally kicked his shoes off while his gray sweat pants fell down to the front of his white socks. His black shirt clung around his neck while he moved backwards on the bed, so his feet wouldn't dangle any more.

A lamp was on near the unnoticeable desk that sat in the other corner of the room. Right now she was studying over her last pair of notes. She had been studying for about an hour. During that time, he relaxed on the gracious bed. He did get up a couple of times to get a glass of water from the kitchen. Other than that, he stayed implanted on the bed.

He closed his eyes after feeling the darkness from the storm. The lights were turned off, once in a blue moon, to her dismay. He would stare at the stars, the ones that rested on her ceiling. When the lights appeared again, she went back to studying. She rested her head on her right hand while her elbow made a permanent mark on the desk. Her blonde hair fell down and kept tapping her forearm every now and then. She would move it away before parting her hair. He would notice this and smirk each time in amusement. She looked so magnificent when she did it. He would examine the ceiling fan, which was blue in color. The color became unclear after watching it for more than five minutes. He could only see the wings of the airplane, so he imagined. With each breath, his eyes started to form a new vision. The wings started to fly so frantically and so fast that he couldn't keep up with it. He closed his eyes. When reopening them, he engaged upon the fan again. Sure enough, it was a blue fan.

Country music still occurred in the background. After the classic annoyance of the commentators, they finally played a song. Of course, it was a song he didn't know. He didn't take much to country, although she did. She would sing almost every song. He didn't care for any kind of music; however, he went along with country for her. He didn't hate country with the utmost attitude like some people did. He just didn't have any music to call his own.

Another twenty minutes passed and nothing changed. He wasn't growing impatient, just getting tired. He was ready to sleep or go. He looked around the room, before bringing his attention back to her. Sure enough, she was still parting her hair like before. She couldn't refrain from resting her right hand on her head. Her elbow was about two feet deep from being planted on the desk.

"I think I'm going…I think it's time."

"You don't have to leave," she replied. He knelt over while putting on his shoes. He didn't do it at the speed he was used to. He looked up at her as she walked over to him. She knelt down next to him, while he paused with his shoes.

"I want you to stay."

"No…it's okay. You're doing your studying and school work. I'll…go ahead and get going. I'll see you…tomorrow."

He rose to his feet after finishing his last shoe. He noticed that he hadn't tied them; therefore, he bent back down smiling foolishly. He took his time. He still messed up a couple of times. Finally he got it right after the third try.

"I'm almost done. I'm done. I want you to stay."

"No. It's okay…I…" he started; however, she interrupted him because a country song came over the radio. It was her favorite song. It was their song. It may as well have been his song. He sat down on the bed while she walked over to him, dancing during the duration of her walk. She did a clumsy country line dance to him. He could only laugh at her.

"It's a great day to be alive…" She started to sing while she grabbed his hands with hers. She brought him up; however, he didn't want to dance. He sat back down, but she brought him up again while holding him close. He managed to bring his left arm out after placing his right hand around her waist.

"I got a three-day beard and I don't plan to shave," Carter expressed the words with the song. She smiled as she placed her left hand on his unhopeful face. She ran it across three times before giving him a kiss. They continued to slow dance. He would surprise her by spinning her out and bringing her back.

"A little trick I learned."

This may have been the only country song he liked. It was because of her, and, any time this song came on, she wanted to dance like now. This was their song. When they had their first date, he had said, "It's a great day to be alive." She insisted that was her favorite song. Although he wasn't much of a dancer, he still made a good impression.

He spun her around again before bringing her back to him. He swung her out and spun her back three times as he held her close yet again. She laughed the entire time while expressing gratitude. She was extremely happy with him. "You just know what to do, don't you?"

"I might grow me a fu man chu and it's a great day…to be alive."

"What did I do to you?"

"You made me happy," he replied. He spun her out again, before bringing her back for the very end of the song. They continued to hold each other even with the announcer speaking in the background. He was going to stop dancing; however, she urged him to keep going. He moved backwards, heading for the bed, but she pulled him back as soon as the next song started. She kept singing. She was actually a decent singer. It was her voice that brought him back.

"If I had two dozen roses…"

"You know I meet with the doctors tomorrow?"

She didn't reply to his statement. She kept singing and dancing while he spun her out again; however, this time, when he brought her back, he stopped her during her third spin. He held her from behind as he started to walk around the room with her while she laughed. She turned her head back and gave him a kiss. They brought the dance back to their original position.

"I'm scared."

"Don't be. I'm sure everything will be okay."

The song ended, as did their dance. He sat on the bed while she studied for ten more minutes. During the tenth minute, she was cut off from studying because of a question.

"What if it doesn't work out?"

"What?"

"What if everything…everything goes wrong? It seems that way. What if it doesn't work out?" Carter asked while he sat up on her bed. Once again he started to put his shoes on. She didn't reply to his question. She sat there in shock wondering why he would ask it. Carter didn't see the problem with the question; therefore, he kept putting his shoes on after missing several times. "I'm just going to go…I will see you tomorrow." She exited her chair in a panic while Carter walked towards the door. She broke in front of him. He didn't have a smirk or a smile. His face stood motionless. Her face became tearful; however, it was the most sincere look he had ever seen.

"If it doesn't work out, then it doesn't work out, but right now we're here. I'm here, and it's tonight. Don't leave." Carter sighed while looking away tearfully. He brought his smile back towards her after faint seconds. He placed his right hand on her face as he parted her hair; he was imitating her from earlier.

"So your mother was involved in an accident?" the doctor asked.

Carter finished drinking his third glass of water. The doctor offered to refill it; however, Carter waved his hand back and forth, saying "no." "My mother…there's a story right there. I could probably write an entire book on my mother…ha; well, a lot of people, well, doctors, said my mother has some disorder. I don't remember what it is, and I should know…I mean, she is my mother…ha, not by choice. But she's stuck in the past, all the time it seems, and when she's not…she surprises the hell out of me. I don't believe the doctors though, because…she was always like this, well, since I was thirteen, not just four years ago. She never went to a doctor though…until four years ago."

"What kind of accident?"

"She was in a car wreck, and she hit her head…concussion. She wasn't wearing her hat that day…and that's why she thinks the accident happened…haha…oh, my mother. They took her to the hospital, did the head scan and everything. She's crazy…ha, well, I don't mean that in a mean way."

"Of course not."

"I just can't relate to my mothe r…at all. I could when I was younger, but after giving up on my father…my mother didn't, and so I couldn't relate to her anymore."

"Why did you give up on your father?"

"I saw how crazy it made my mother," Carter replied. He took a sigh while closing his eyes. "I can still envision it. It's still there. It's imprinted in my mind."

The bags were packed, and the fish were stacked, tackled, and ready to go. The sea was calling for them. His beard was thick, just like his four partners. Their boat was called "Glacis," which didn't make much sense to the thirteen-year-old boy who watched his father pack supplies. His father tossed them effortlessly from the deck to the fishing boat. The thirteen-year-old boy held a football in his right hand, and he would toss it in the air every time his father tossed a package onto the boat. He would drop the ball every time he tossed it in the air. He wasn't a very good catch like his father was. His father would teach him how to do it after his fishing trip. It would only be a one-month trip, maybe two or three days longer.

His mother was biding a goodbye to her husband. She hugged him, for months it seemed, before he finally broke the hug. He walked over to his son. He rubbed his son's illustrious hair with his right hand. His son was full of energy now.

"Dad, dad, you're going to teach me when you get back, right? You're going to teach me?"

"Sure, son. You already have the arm. Keep throwing it through that tire over there. I even put a rope on it if you want to swing it around and try." He picked up his son and held him. His son dropped the football while clinging to his father's neck. His father's smile grew with intensity. He kissed his son's forehead before placing him back on God's sweet earth. They waved goodbye from the deck and watched them pass the lighthouse at eight in the morning. The boy waved for the entire time as he held his football in his right hand. He waved with his left hand even after the boat was out of sight. His mother placed her arm around his shoulder and led him inside for the usual breakfast, oatmeal.

Every day that kid was outside throwing that football through that tire. After weeks of trying it with the rope, he finally did it, and he jumped for joy. He looked around for someone to watch. There was no one; therefore, he would look out into the water for his father's boat. There would be no sign of luck today.

Then he was no longer thirteen; he was seventeen, in high school. He didn't hang out with anyone or participate in anything. He went home after school every day. When he was sixteen, he would go wait by the shore for a while and walk the rusty deck; however, after he was sixteen, he never waited again.

He ran around a tree, his body fit from weights, push-ups, sit-ups, crunches, and boxing with the boxing bag for days. He ran around another dream-diminishing tree. His breath was hard as the football stayed in his right hand as he ran around another tree. The tire swung from side to side at a frantic pace. He came around the fourth tree ready to throw. He planted his feet before throwing a bullet that went straight through the tire. He put a dent in the shed after scorching the defense.

After the workout, he went inside to cool off; however, his mother would continue to walk around the house and do stupid activities. She wouldn't even explain herself anymore. Usually she waited on top of the lighthouse at night. She would wear a crappy hat and wait. He walked up there occasionally. Sometimes he brought his mother a drink, although she wouldn't answer to anything he said, unless it related to his father of course.

Football season came. Practice was conducted on a normal basis. When the games came, he watched from the visitor's stand by himself. He would watch every mistake from the home team quarterback. He had all his stats memorized, and the stats were a horrible sight. Each time he sarcastically smirked when he heard someone at school comment on how good the high school quarterback was. He thought it was funny when people thought he was good.

"Why didn't you play?"

"I didn't want to…I guess."

The doctor shook his head "no" while sliding over a new glass of water for Carter. Carter eloquently sipped it with a grin. He placed it back down on the table. "Why did you count his stats if you didn't want to play? You were better than him, weren't you?" Carter nodded.

"You didn't play because of your father?"

"My mother."

"You think you could have played great?"

"I don't know…doesn't really matter, does it?"

The grass field was a sight that no one should go without seeing. Today it was in beautiful condition. It was before game day. He stood out on the field by himself watching the amazing weather circulate the balanced field. He graciously looked around the stadium while he brought his head up towards the stands. He smirked because he could see himself making an impact on this field. The sun was out and it was cool, seventy degrees, perfect football weather; however, the moment didn't last long. The football players coming onto the field interrupted him. They tried to harass him off the field although he didn't budge until the starting quarterback came over along with his friends, his overweight offensive line. They moved him out the way, but he continued to watch. The coach wasn't out yet; therefore, all of the players messed around. They would go through the all the routine plays. Their white jerseys matched the color of the goal line. That's where he stood right now. The quarterback stood on the fifteen as he tried to throw a deep cross towards his receiver; however, it fell at his feet after a forty-yard route.

A bag of footballs rested about ten yards to his right. He walked over towards the bag and grabbed out a football while holding it down next to his waist. The receiver ran back to the huddle yelling at the quarterback to get it to him. He was an all-state receiver; therefore, he wanted to make his yards this year. The deep routes would be the way to do it. He ran it again. Once again the quarterback didn't make it. The receiver would continue to complain as the quarterback threw a check down on the next play.

"HEY! Run that route again," Carter yelled as he stood twenty yards behind the line of scrimmage. The next play started; Carter imitated the starting quarterback by pretending to hike the ball. The coach walked out during this time as he made it past the bleachers. The receiver took off on his post route again. Before making the cut, Carter threw the ball while everyone watched, the coach included. It sailed towards the receiver. It fell right into his hands. He took off and headed towards the end zone. Cheers came from the sideline while Carter smiled at the quarterback. He gave Carter one of the most hideous looks in the world. He threw that ball sixty yards, and the very next play Carter bulleted the ball forty yards to a man crossing across the middle of the field. The coach approached him; however, Carter put down the ball he had just picked up. He walked by the coach with a playful smile. "Sorry if I interrupted your practice." He didn't say another word. He walked away without answering the coach's question.

"So why did you go down there?"

"Ha…to show them what they were missing."

The doctor leaned forward again while Carter took another drink from the glass of water. The glass was almost empty again. Carter evaporated water on a regular basis. That was his thing. If you put a glass or bottled water in front of him, he would drink it vigorously.

"What did he ask you?"

"My name. So…why aren't you smiling in your picture?"

"Excuse me?"

"Your picture…on your desk…ha, you're not smiling, and everyone else is," Carter replied. He turned the picture towards the doctor while the doctor looked it over. He reluctantly shook his head in agreement.

"I'm not a picture person."

"Yeah, me neither," Carter replied as he scratched his neck. He continued to study the picture as if it were an upcoming midterm. "Empty desk…cabinets…a reminder, not smiling." Carter would have kept going but he looked up at the doctor in the middle of his sentence while smiling.

"I'm separated."

"Right, sorry," Carter replied as he placed the picture back in its original position. His smile evaporated just like the water. He waited for the doctor to say something.

"Don't be. It wasn't your fault."

"What happened?" Carter asked.

The doctor finally sighed like Carter. He rubbed his chin a couple of times before yawning. His yawn triggered Carter's. Carter glanced at the clock during the end of his yawn. It wouldn't be dark for a while, so everything was okay. "I don't know. Why does anything end? It wasn't much. Just a lot…"

"Of little things. I know…all about that. Maybe not to your extent, but I do. It's the little things that kill you."

The cool air fell on top of the gassy hill. The wishing well must have been at least twenty yards away from the snow-colored blanket. It was a white blanket spread out over the grass. He could see the ocean shore from this hill while he sat underneath an apple tree, which reached over the clouds it seemed. Leaves fell from the tree with each indication of a wind change. Two apples rested on the blanket, as did he.

The blue sky turned to velvet as the sun went down. The clouds covered every inch of the sky; however, no cloud appeared dreadful. His legs became cold from that particular wind change. He only wore a pair of blue basketball shorts, although he did have a white long sleeved shirt on with a gray shirt over it. His socks stretched up to his knees. He felt goofy for wearing them; however, goofy may have been his best aspect right now. His glasses were clean. Anyone could see his or her reflection. Right now he was waiting for someone, one person to come and see him. This hill was one of those places where all life would be stopped for one moment, just for him.

He would sleep up here if he could, except it was too cold for him. He did sleep up on the hill one night with Casey. That was a great night. A night like that usually only happened once, because if it happened again, it took away the spark and magic from that one night. That one night would come again some day. It would remind him of all life's changes, the growing up, and aging from childhood to adulthood. Just like New York.

She walked up the hill while her blonde hair swayed from side to side. She had a white flower tucked in her hair, and it looked gorgeous as the sunrise. Her blue eyes could be seen from a distance. He thought the ocean water was coming his way. She wasn't dressed up in an outfit that some called classy. She was in a pair of shorts, with a regular Jet's shirt. He grabbed her hand and helped her sit down while she leaned against his chest. She gave him a kiss; however, it wasn't a normal peck like lately. It consisted of passion, so much heart. He brushed her hair back behind her neck while he tipped the flower behind her left ear. He couldn't help but smile again. Then he gave her something important. It was a notebook. Only four pages consisted of writing. She didn't look in it after he handed it to her.

"I want you to have this. I spoke with the doctors today...and this right here...is what I think of everything. Don't read it now, but later...much later. Okay?" He gave her another kiss while she nodded in approval. He moved her hair back again while they both leaned back against the tender grass. She looked at his left wrist and noticed his watch was gone, the watch she gave him a while back. He loved that watch.

"What happened to your watch?"

"Oh...I don't know. Uh...I guess I forgot it. That a problem?"

"No," she replied. She held his hand while darkness fell. They watched the night sky, but no words really occurred. She held his hand while she rested her head on his chest. He would run his fingers through her signature hair. After a while, they covered up with the other half of the blanket as they continued to watch the night sky. Every night consisted of the love between them. It was never stated from his side though. She knew how he felt though. He still after all this time couldn't manage to say it.

It mattered to him because there was a reason the watch was forgotten. He wanted to tell her something that night, but the night was content. He didn't want to ruin it with the conversation he had planned. It would come at a later day. The watch was just a little thing; however, in actuality it might have been the biggest in the world. It made the point that little things are always shown first.

The glass of water was finished. Carter was back in the restroom again in front of the mirror looking at himself. He kept throwing water on his face at a consistent pace. He turned off the water while closing his eyes. He awoke from the sink minutes later. He covered his face with water again after opening his eyes. He wiped his hands and face before walking outside. When he returned to the clammy room, the doctor was absent again. He walked over to the bookshelf while waiting for the doctor to come back. He looked through all the medical books, one at a time.

"So the watch was a little thing?" the doctor asked while he walked into the room. He stood next to the window. Carter didn't face him. He kept flipping through the row of books, and then he came to the relationship books, which tried to reconcile marriages together.

"It was a little thing because it was a reminder." Carter held the reconcile marriage book out to the side before finding another and another. He placed them back on the bookshelf while the doctor watched. He didn't say anything to Carter. He was fine with him looking through his belongings. He was a little uncomfortable about Carter asking him family questions though.

"A reminder of what?"

"A reminder of what I would be leaving behind. A reminder that it wasn't just me…who was hurting. Ha…and here I thought I was trying to save her."

"Save her from what?"

Carter turned around and walked back to his seat. The doctor did the same while Carter coughed down towards the floor. "Save her from hurt…pain, and me. I wasn't thinking…of her…I was thinking about me…which was wrong."

"What happened next?"

CHAPTER 4

▼

INSURRECTION

"What lies behind us and what lies before us are small matters compared to what lies within us."

—Ralph Waldo Emerson

It didn't happen all at once. It didn't happen during the blink of an eye either. It was days of the same consistency, and, after four days, she caught on. It was one step at a time. That was his plan before hitting her with the big finale. He wasn't going to have her wait on him hand and foot. He didn't want to be a burden on her even though he thought of her day and night. He couldn't do it anymore. It was how he felt.

Every day, every minute on every hour, he would do little things purposely. He was hoping she would take the hint, but she didn't. She was there through the bad and the good, although he didn't want her to be there with him, to watch him suffer through the bad. He didn't call her. He didn't answer the door, questions, or even smile, as he always did. His personality changed, as did his lifestyle. His attitude towards everything changed in a matter of weeks. Everyone remembers the little things. No one remembers the moments when love breaks barriers, or when love carries someone through a tragic time. It's the little things that define a person. It's always the little things that end up being mentioned after a breakup, ending, or death.

How she thought seventy-five degrees was cold. How she hated soup; however, she would still drink a hot cup of it whenever she was sick. How she loved the song "A Great Day to Be Alive" even though she couldn't stand Travis Tritt. She would always have to sing and dance to it with him, even to his displeasure.

Or how he would get her a rose on a regular day, any day. It didn't matter about the occasion, yet he forgot her birthday. How he would never ask for directions when driving, like most men do. How he smiled even when nothing funny was mentioned. There was nothing funny around. It was a defense mechanism that went off whenever he was nervous.

Chemo was over, treatment too, radiation therapy, and it was done. He didn't want to do it anymore. It was over. He gave up. She knew it and she wasn't going to try and talk him out of it either. What was there to do now? That's the question that wandered through his mind. Maybe he could do something memorable before he went; however, that wasn't his forte. He wasn't one to do something extraordinary even if it was in his best interest. He wanted to be alone, which wasn't something he should be doing. He should have been with friends, family, loved ones, but he was alone for a specific reason. He never explained his reason. He felt he didn't have to. It should have been something they already knew.

It was a beautiful day, it really was, and the word beautiful was an understatement to how it looked outside. The sun stretched across the blue sky while white clouds resembled the marshmallow man. The ocean water broke wave after wave after wave. It brought in so much life.

"Are you there? Are you here…right now? If you are…I sincerely hope…I do, I hope that you do exist. I'm not one to do this. I never have…I don't know why. Praying isn't one of my strong suits. Praying isn't something I did…but then again. You know that. I've been thinking about things. Thinking about life in general. Why you do things in your own way. But…why? That may seem like a stupid question to you, but to me…it's one of those questions that are stuck in my mind. I could try and figure it out, but then again, I can't figure out something I don't understand. Ha…it took something like this, for me to pray…I'm not saying I believe, I'm not saying I don't. I don't know what to believe. But I know what to do…and I got you to thank for that, don't I? Thanks…you know the way I mean it too."

His eyes opened as they tweaked around the room. He took another sip from his bottle of liquor. He sat in the corner of his room, blinds closed, light turned off, and the room was a mess. He sat in the corner in the same outfit from the other night. It was the shorts, long-sleeved undershirt. He had on the stained gray shirt over the top that consisted of a rotten liquor smell. Every two seconds he would say something before taking a drink. He never drank; however, he figured there wasn't anything wrong with it now. He wasn't drinking to drink. He was drinking to get drunk. He kept drinking the night away as he held onto the bottle tight. He wouldn't budge from his grip.

The devil's darkness set in. His face couldn't be seen. After the third drink, he hid his face between his knees; therefore, the darkness covered his entire body. The bottle, half gone, now rested on the floor next to his right foot while his cries carried across the room. She heard this while she stood outside the door. She caught on to the avoiding for the past four days. She hesitated to enter the room. This was the first time he acted this way. He wasn't the same person anymore; therefore, he wasn't the person certain people grew to love and respect.

At night, the wind picked up fiercely. It forced its way against the doors of the lighthouse while waves broke over the rocks, splashing against the side of the lighthouse. His mother at the time didn't move from her spot. Every night after seven she would do the same thing. Tonight was no different. She held onto her hat as she talked to herself on a consistent basis. All and all though, he didn't budge from his grip on life. He continued to drink while sitting in the corner. He cried one breath at a time.

This wasn't him. He knew it, which is why he was crying. He couldn't break this new form of life. He was doing it for a reason. It was a reason of far greater cause. It would help her move away from him, leave him alone, because he was tired of leaning on her, using her. He was tired of watching her suffer while he went through his entire ordeal everyday.

The smell of alcohol penetrated not only his clothes but also his breath. It crept over to the door. The atrocious smell made its way under the doorway while she stood outside. The smell from outside no longer consisted of fish. The wind was too strong. His mother sipped her hot cup of tea with pleasure as she closed the last window. She proceeded downstairs and walked down the numerous steps leading to the hallway. That's where she noticed Casey. Casey still stood outside the door, wearing her blue sweater, which Carter loved.

She didn't know what to do. It had been more than twenty minutes that she stood outside this room. Carter's mother walked down the hallway swaying from side to side while sipping her hot cup of tea. She had a routine. Casey leaned against the door to hear. She tried to make a decision as Carter's mother walked by with no concern. She didn't say a word.

He took another sip of the dreadful liquor before placing the bottle back on the floor. Two seconds later he picked it up again and took another carefree drink. His mind was made up. Nothing could change it even after taking the daredevil drink. He held the bottle in his right hand, near his chest. His crying ceased while he focused on another bottle, smaller than the liquor bottle. It was a bottle of sleeping pills. He poured them into the palm of his hand. He couldn't do it. He threw them across the room realizing how stupid that idea was.

"What have you got me doing here? Huh…is this what you wanted? If so…I hate you," he tearfully implied as he threw the bottle of liquor across the room. It broke against the wall about eight feet in front of him. He started to cry again. By this time, Casey entered the room. Finally a shed of light was brought into the room. It reached over to his knees; however, his head was still hidden.

"Carter. Carter," she repeated again.

This time she was too sympathetic for his liking. She took her time walking over to him. He looked up at her with his eyes drooping from the alcohol. He finally spoke while she stopped in her tracks. "What are you doing here?"

"Carter. You know the answer to that."

"Go…I want you to leave. Okay?…go, just go." He stuck his head back down between his knees while she waited for him to say something.

"Just go…GO. I don't want you here."

She went against his words as she took another step towards him; however, he finally brought his head up. "Get out of here. I need to be left alone."

She did. Then it was two days later, then four, and then a week. Soon it would be two weeks. No communication occurred between the two even though she tried. He separated himself from her. It was over. He thought he was doing her a favor by doing this; however, she would keep trying. He wouldn't have any of it. After a while, she stopped trying to contact him. She gave him his wish. He felt relieved, although, as the end came closer, he started to feel guilty. He felt alone.

Another month went by. He stayed at the forsaken lighthouse with his mother. Of course, once in awhile his mother would surprise him by saying something that actually made sense. She would ask him to talk to someone because she noticed her son was acting depressed; however, she would always counter with something so cynical. "Talk to your father."

He hated that expression more than anything. He hated it more than death. Life was different for him without Casey. He was without his light of hope. He would sit inside his room all day reading a book. Or he would go sit up on the hill where he once shared great moments with her. Now he was alone on that hill and he would do things he never thought he would do. He walked over to the wishing well in which he would drop numerous amounts of dimes. He even made a wish, although the wish wasn't for him. It was for her. He couldn't take his mind off of her no matter how hard he tried.

He figured he would get over it in time, although he didn't. As his condition worsened, he felt alone. He wanted to call her. He should have. He couldn't manage the strength to do it after what he did. He grew tired every day and would sleep most of the day. Some days, he couldn't even manage his way out of bed. His mother wouldn't be much help. The phone would lie next to him. All he had to do was call and she would have come. One day he picked up the phone and dialed four numbers; however, after that fourth number, he stopped. He started to cry while he tried to get out of bed. His body movements wouldn't keep up; therefore, he would fall to floor.

"Why didn't you call her?"

"I didn't…because…I didn't want her to see me…at my weakest point."

Carter finished his fourth glass of water. Instead of placing it back on the desk where the doctor could refill it, he placed it on the floor next to the recorder. The doctor's eyes shifted over towards Carter. He finally took notice that they were blue eyes. The doctor got up and fixed his coat on his coat rack. Carter started to laugh. "What's so funny?"

"If anything was out of place…she would do the same thing."

"So you do miss her?"

"You miss anyone you love…don't you?" Carter replied as he pulled his attention towards the picture. The doctor nodded along. Carter coughed before getting up from his seat. He didn't need a break though. He stretched, not long, kind of like stretching while getting out of bed after a nap. He walked over to the bookshelf again.

"I love books. How they all tell a story…about…love, life, the journey, because that's what it's about, right? The journey…never the ending. It's about the work they put in to it…how it started…how they first met…how there was a lasting impression."

The doctor rose from his chair as he walked around the desk. He stood next to the window. "How did you first meet Casey?" Carter took his time while he put the question on hold. He looked at the row of books, he took one in his palm, and then he put it back again just like he had done before.

"Oh…oh, I was cocky. Ha…oh yeah, and I was trying to impress her. I filled in for a friend at his college…for intramural football, and we played against her team…and I noticed her because she was beautiful…I wondered why she was playing football." He took a sigh while picking up another book. "I must have thrown eight…nine touchdowns, and the last three were on her, because…ha…I would show my smile to her and give her a nod, and…I thought I was catching her attention…when I did. I threw the ball right over her head, and we score d...and each time walking down the field...I would say something sarcastic or funny to her. Oh, I was cocky."

The grass field wasn't like the football field he once threw on to impress the coach or the quarterback of high school. It was a place for fun. It was a park on the main street of Long Island. Carter's team was winning all game long. Of course, the reason why would be the hot hand from Carter. He would rub it in too while he ran around the field, being chased by three or four people each time. He would throw off one foot. The football would land right into the receiver's hand for a touchdown.

He would laugh while he walked up the occupied field. He would notice the blonde woman with blue eyes. He would smirk at her while he walked past and he would ask, "What's your name?"

She wouldn't answer; however, his consistent amount of asking would bring a laugh to her face. She would give him a pat on the back for trying. He watched her while she walked back to her side of the field awaiting the kickoff. She wore a pair of short shorts, tank top, with a football jersey covering it. It was a jersey for the Jets and he despised the Jets. He was a New York Giants' fan, New York's finest. It showed by the shirt he was wearing. It was a gray long-sleeved shirt which said "I Love the Giants." It was painted on the shirt; therefore, he didn't buy it that way.

They played on for another thirty minutes, and each time he burned them for a touchdown, he would ask her a question while smiling. "What's your name? What kind of flowers do you like? How can you not like the Giants? You're from New York, right?" After each question, he would watch her go back to her team. She would start to take a little interest in him because he was so persistent.

After the game, she was packing her things into a blue bag. Another game was going on now, so everyone was watching. He walked over to her so he could start a friendly conversation.

"Hey."

"Hi," she replied while she zipped up her bag. She stood there watching him, already waiting for another question.

"You know...you were kind of getting burned out there today. Now I could give you some pointers," he said. His smile appeared yet again.

"I really have to get going," she replied.

He walked around one of the bleachers so he could catch up. She was 5'5" tall; therefore, she was four inches shorter than he was. He looked down at her and into her eyes while he continued to smile.

"How about I take you out to a movie, or...anywhere?"

"I'm sorry. I'm just not looking for a date or a good time right now," she replied. She wasn't being sincere with her answer. He noticed because her eyes shifted away from him during the duration of her answer.

"Well, what if I promise you a horrible time?"

"You're really persistent, aren't you? Just full of yourself," she replied. She laughed as she gently slapped his arm.

"Not really full of myself, just confident. There's a small difference…so I take it the answer is a 'yes'?"

"I don't even know your name."

"Carter."

The time shifted again. The session was half done. He knew it, and during this time he was washing his face in the bathroom. He looked into the mirror; his face was incredibly pale, and his smile didn't have the charm it once had. He tried to notice something familiar about himself. He missed the past because that's all he had. The future wasn't there for him anymore. Every happy memory he ever thought about or brought up had to do with her.

The cold Colorado weather was outside. The inside was breached with heat from the warm fire. They drove from New York to Colorado during winter break. The snow rested outside while they toasted marshmallows inside next to the fire. He held her in his arms as they swayed to the music. They both had exams right after this break, although right now it wasn't on their minds. This was their moment to get away from everything. This was their night.

They went skiing earlier in the day. Carter never did it before. She taught him how, and, after hours of practicing, he finally got it. He was frantic the entire time because he thought he was going to break his leg. He also thought he would crush his face against the side of a tree. He didn't like doing things he didn't know how to do; however, she opened him up for it. Every day in Colorado he tried something new. Her mother lived there; however, they stayed at a resort. They wanted the full vacation experience with each other.

It was a log cabin up in the cold mountains of Aspen, Colorado. Everything was clean, neat, and in its particular place. The only thing in use would be the fireplace. They opened the bag of fluffy marshmallows. He handed her the marshmallow while she cautiously took a bite. He placed another one in the fire as he held her close. He could only relax while she nibbled on his ear.

It was only a two-day stay; however, it was a stay that was memorable because it opened up new doors for their relationship. The drive to Colorado was memorable. They almost hit a deer and then a truck. She was driving at that point. When he took over, the tire was slashed somewhere; therefore, they had to put the spare on. He would listen to her nagging the entire time as he changed the tire. She would explain to him that he was doing it wrong. His comeback phrase was always the same. "Would you like to do it?"

"Nice comeback," she would reply. She would study the map and tell him the wrong directions again. After fixing the tire, he would look at the map already knowing she was wrong. "I am not wrong. I know what I'm doing," she would say.

"You never know what you're doing. Being blonde doesn't help, does it?" he would say numerous times while laughing each time. She would playfully hit him before giving him a kiss. "You know I'm right," she would insinuate.

"No, you're not. I know where we're going."

"Really? Then where are we?"

"We're somewhere between New York and Colorado," he replied. He would laugh again while she pushed his arm. After the tire was secure, they started to drive again while she held the map. "Why don't you give me the map?"

"No. You can't drive and look at the map at the same time."

"Yes, I can. Give me the map," he replied as he reached over for the map; however, she would move it away from his reach. He would stop while she yelled for him to watch the road. He used the power windows to his advantage. It was his diabolical plot. He rolled down the windows. He locked her side of the window even after she expressed, "I'm cold." She kept telling him to roll up the window.

"Give me the map, and I'll roll up the windows."

"Roll up the windows, and I'll tell you what exit to take."

He reached for the map again as he drove around a corner; however, he missed. She kept laughing; however, during her laugh, the map flew out the window. She watched as her face was blushing with redness; however, she kept laughing while he looked over at her with a bitter look. It didn't last long. "You lost the map? Our only map? It's time to put the windows up."

"It's okay. We can stop and get another one."

"I'm not stopping."

"Yes, you are. We can get a map and ask for directions," she replied as she pointed out a gas station coming up on the right side of the road. He drove by the gas station with no intention of pulling over. "What are you doing?"

"I'm not asking for directions."

"Uh. What is it with men and not asking for directions?" He brought his car back down to a good pace before turning around. He headed back for the gas station. She laughed at him and said, "See? I knew I was right. You don't know where you are."

"I do. We need gas," he replied.

"Oh. Okay. Well as long as you know where you're going."

"I do."

He pulled next to one of the pumps at the gas station. The gas cap was on her side of the car. He exited the vehicle while she remained sitting inside and after he picked up the gas pump, he put it back in its holder. He walked over to her window while she opened the door.

"What is it?"

"I have to pay inside first. Be right back," he said. He walked away and headed inside the gas station. She couldn't see inside although she figured he would be right back. After about five minutes of waiting in the car, she was going to get out and go inside; however, he finally came out. He walked over to the driver's side and hopped in.

"What about gas?" she asked. He turned on the car and put it in drive. He drove away. "Oh. We don't need it. I just used the restroom." He tried not to crack a smile. She kept looking at his face while his smile cracked a smidge. "You asked for directions," she exclaimed in an ecstatic way. "I did not." However, he couldn't hold back his smile.

"You liar," she replied as she slapped his arm. He smiled while checking his gas gauge for real this time. Once again he turned around and headed back towards the gas station. "What are you doing now?"

"We really need gas."

That was what the trip consisted of before arriving in Colorado. During their second marshmallow, it started to snow outside. He got up while bringing her with him. He opened the door and watched the snow fall outside. After ten minutes of watching, it stopped. He walked outside while she persistently followed. She was used to this weather when she was growing up because she lived here until she was eight. He loved snow. He picked up a pile of snow while he strategically made it into a snowball. He threw it at her. It connected with her arm. She picked up one of her own which she was going to make nice, packed, and perfect; however, he already connected a second one.

They ran around in the snow throwing snowballs at each other. After she hit him a third time, he fell down purposely. He pretended he was hurt. He waited there for her to come to his aid while she walked over. She was hesitant because she knew he was faking. She was waiting for him to come up and throw a snowball at her. "I could be hurt here and you don't care," he playfully said. She jumped on him right after that comment. She wouldn't let him move while she held both his arms. He didn't fight it. He kissed her while her hair fell into his eyes. After the kiss, he was going to say something to her but before he could, he felt a cold rush smudged onto his head. He slid her off while throwing another snowball at her. She kept running away from him while he chased her down a hill; however, he buckled in the process.

That night they rested in front of the fire. The snow fell, as they both wanted the moment to last longer than it actually did. The moment was nothing more than the two of them in front of a fire, holding on to each other as if it were the last day they would have this time. After tonight, it would go back to reality. It would go back to the hectic drive home. It would be hectic because one way or another she would drive. Her driving wasn't a pretty sight. That night consisted of love at its finest moment; even if the words weren't expressed, their actions were. The lights shut off as they both left the fire scene and went to another one.

Carter opened the door. He entered the silent room where the doctor waited. The curtains were closed now because Carter grew irritated a while ago. The young receptionist kept peeking inside. The light was dim to Carter while his eyes adjusted to the room. Everything faded as he walked over to his chair.

"So I take it you made a good impression on her? And you got your date?"

"Ha…actually no. I didn't get a date. Just a name. I met up with her at a later date…and I had to be persistent just to get her to have a cup of coffee with me."

He sat down on a small couch with friends from the intramural football game at a local coffee shop. His teammates would depart; however, he would stay. The set up wasn't very spectacular. Only two couches and about five tables occupied the entire coffee shop. It was a very tiny establishment, although they served the best coffee around. He was sitting alone, drinking his coffee. After about twenty minutes of reading the paper, he was going to leave. He was wearing a pair of his basketball shorts again, a blue long-sleeved undershirt with a white shirt over it, which was a Giants shirt, of course. He was going to play another game in about two hours; therefore, he was already dressed for the part.

His blue Giants hat rested next to the rest of the newspaper. He only read the sports page. He read that as the door opened. He noticed a familiar woman. An energetic smile came to his face as she walked over to the counter and asked for a coffee. She turned around and noticed him immediately. His enduring smile was noticeable; however, he picked up his paper. He pretended to read.

"How are you a Giants fan?" she asked seconds later.

Her skirt stopped at her knees. She wore a pink button-down shirt that stopped at her waist. She was dressed incredibly nicely. Her hair was curled and her face was covered with the perfect amount of makeup.

"Where are you headed?"

"I have a job interview."

"You want to sit down?" he asked seconds later. He moved his hat away from her side of the table. Her coffee was ready. She turned around and didn't say a word to him; therefore, he didn't know the answer. He picked up his paper, pretending to read again. He stopped while she sat down across from him. He folded the paper, or tried, but it wouldn't work. After he couldn't do it, he tossed it to the side.

"Hi."

"Hi," she replied with her engaging smile. Her dimples showed while he pointed them out.

"So how about the date?"

"You're not going to give that up, are you?"

"Nope," he replied as he took another sip of his coffee. He moved the papers out of the way because the sports section kept unfolding next to his arm. He placed them on the floor while he awaited an answer.

"I'm going to an art gallery this Friday."

"Is that an invitation?" he replied with his dimwitted smile.

"You know what? Yeah, it is. I want you to come. It's right across the street at seven. I'll meet you there."

He was actually surprised that she asked; therefore, he didn't know how to answer at first. He would muster out the right amount of words. He would look forward to their date because he really took an interest in her.

"Okay. I'll see you there. Friday, right?"

"Yes. And my father would love to meet you."

"Father?" he replied quickly while she exited her chair. "Yes. My father. He's in town. I promise a horrible time." She walked away with a sarcastic laugh while leaving the humble establishment. He took another drink of his coffee after stretching his shirt down in confusion.

Carter placed another book back on the bookshelf before walking back to his seat. He felt tired. He took another sip from the water glass, hoping it would give him a refreshing feeling.

"Ha…my first date with her…if you can consider it a date…was meeting her father…oh, that was funny. Ha…she never got to meet mine."

"What happened to your father?"

Carter didn't answer. He walked around the room; however, his attention was on the bookshelf again. He noticed a few cassette tapes on the bottom shelf. He knelt down while looking them over. He didn't take notice of two of the tapes; however, the last one he did. It was a Tim McGraw cassette. He brought it over towards the desk and then sat down after placing it down on the table.

"You a Tim fan?"

"No."

"Yeah, me neither…but there was this one song, and I've heard it recently, and that one song alone…has made me fall in love with country…and his music. It's funny…how one song…can explain how you feel…you know, change how you feel on certain…aspects of life."

He picked up the cassette tape. He looked it over for about ten seconds before sliding it over to the doctor. The doctor picked it up. He put the tape inside one of his drawers without even acknowledging the tape. Carter waited for him to say something; finally the doctor did.

"'She's My Kind of Rain.' That was our song."

"It's a good song."

Carter coughed, no differently than the last time. He took a long drink from his glass of water. He placed it on the floor again next to the tape recorder. "I really like the song…'Live like you were dying'…it was…a good song."

"I haven't heard it."

"Well, I'm not going to sing it to you," Carter replied. Carter coughed reluctantly while trying to gather himself.

"You want more water?"

"I'm fine. You should listen to that song…it explains a lot. Ha…uh…where were we? Oh, that's right. My father."

CHAPTER 5

▼

BEST WISHES

"Most people are other people. Their thoughts are someone else's opinions, their lives a mimicry, their passions a quotation."

—Oscar Wilde

A thought of hope doesn't really consist of much in today's world. It's usually expressed every day. The hope is never fulfilled; therefore, it leaves the feeling of pain. So why would his hope be any different? Waiting for someone to show up after the search has been called off, it wasn't much hope to hope after all. It doesn't make much sense when things go wrong, especially when it deliberately occurs over and over. The thirteen-year-old boy stood alone with his hands empty on the vengeful shores of Long Island. The football from his hand dropped to the ground after hearing the news of his father. The search for him went on for a week, but it appeared the ocean took him. They found the fishing boat, unoccupied. There was never a clear-cut explanation given to him as to why his father was gone. There really wasn't one to signify the ending for his father. No one had the real story.

He didn't talk to anyone after the events of his father. His mother wanted to be left alone as well. She gave herself that privilege. She left herself reminders of her husband throughout the empty lighthouse. At first, Carter thought she did it for him, so he would have reminders of his father; however, that wasn't the case.

It was for her only. After the years went by, Carter got over it, even though he still had a great feeling of emptiness inside. His mother always had her moments or days in which she appeared normal, where she would actually care about her son, but, other than those moments, she never shook from her unfailing past.

His father was a good father, in his opinion, even though his father was rarely home because of fishing trips. The times he was home, he played with his son. He gave him advice. He didn't really give him great advice; however, just communication with your son can mean the world to him. Just listening to the son's energetic ideas while going along with all his games made his day.

He would take his son fishing even though his son hated fishing. He would love to spend time with his father even if it was on a fishing trip. Most of the time, Carter would yell for his father to go fishing with him because he knew his father wouldn't turn it down. Therefore, he would get to spend hours with his father alone on a quiet lake, sometimes even out in the unprotected ocean. His mother was fine in the beginning, with his father around. He didn't know this, but she would take her medication every day. She would always worry about her son on those fishing trips as well. She loved watching her two men go out and come back with fish. Carter would come back with a small fish no bigger than his hand; however, he would tell the story as if he caught a shark and his father would go along with it. His father would pretend to be the hideous shark during their presentation.

There really wasn't a fonder memory of his father. His memory didn't stretch beyond those fishing trips. His mother never told him stories about his father. He could only look at the pictures growing up and make up a story. He only hoped it would be remotely close to the real thing.

After his father was gone, two years later, he would search for clues throughout the house. He would look into information about his father because his mother would be no help. He looked through drawers and found pictures of him, his father, although he didn't remember anything about the certain picture. He could imagine his father, while putting together some kind of interesting story.

His life story would always change from week to week. His imagination would always run wild while changing certain aspects of his life. Finally after turning seventeen, he gave up on those fantasy memories. He realized that he didn't have any. He dealt with it after accepting it. He decided to make new memories on his own. They would be memories for the future, with someone else.

The story of his father was in the papers. His death certificate was finalized, even to the mother's dismay. She wouldn't believe it. She waited even while Carter was accepted into college. He didn't receive congratulations from his mother. He turned down many colleges, many out of state. He didn't want to leave his mother alone. Even though he ignored her entirely anyway, he knew she couldn't live on her own.

"So everything changed after your father?"

"Everything always changes. It would have changed…one way or another. It has to…it's life, right?"

"Is that why you stopped treatment? You wanted to make another change?"

"I wanted to live out my remaining days…without pain," Carter replied. He rubbed his eyes during his small yawn. He brought his sleeves up to his wrist again; however, this time they stayed there. This surprised him.

"How did the change help you?"

"It didn't," Carter sarcastically implied. He laughed along with his sarcastic tone.

He fell out of bed while the alarm clock buzzed on for at least another thirty seconds. During the process of the alarm, he tried to get up but couldn't. He couldn't even do a push-up right now. He could unplug the alarm; therefore, he yanked it out of the wall with the remaining strength he had left. His room was completely dark. He could hear the newspapers rustle while he tried to get up. He grew frustrated by the crackling of the newspapers. He kept pushing them away in irritation. "Damn it!"

He gave up when he told everyone he wasn't doing treatment anymore. After coming home to sleep, he couldn't even get out of bed. Of course, that passed after minutes of small moves. After those small moves, the sensation in his legs came back. He made it to the couch in his study where he would pick up a book. He did something familiar even if he did it alone. He turned on the radio. He made sure it was on the country station before sitting down. He would hear a song that he actually knew. She would sing this country song every time it came on the radio.

His sweat pants rested on the couch while his light blue long-sleeved shirt clung to his neck. He rolled the sleeves up to his forearms. The country music wasn't turned up very loud, although it was at a level at which he could hear it. It didn't go any further than the simple room. He didn't even know why he was sitting, listening to the same old country music. Then he realized why when he had a picture of her in his hand. He wanted to call. He didn't. He just held the picture.

Then there was another familiar song that came over the radio. He actually knew this one. It meant something to him. There was a costume party one night, and they both went to it. He had on a great costume while her costume wasn't a costume at all. He showed up in scrubs, pretending to be a doctor. He even had the stethoscope around his neck.

She wore a dress. The dress was amazing on her. It was bright red and it stopped at her feet. She didn't know it was a costume party. He told her she looked beautiful for the event. The costume party wasn't anything special; in one case it may have been; however, it was just a simple college dance. They listened to music while they danced. During their dance, they shared their first kiss.

It didn't happen in the middle of a sentence. It happened at the end of sequence of sentences. It wasn't even coming from something he made up. It came from a song. The song was well written. He would sing certain parts of the song while they slow danced in a room full of strangers who all wore terrifying costumes.

"Never could build you a castle." He smiled while she leaned in. She placed her head near his right shoulder. She withdrew it seconds later because he kept singing the words to the song. He looked right at her, as if he was stating something true.

"Some people think I'm a loser. Cause I seldom get things right. But you make me feel like a winner. When you wrap me in your arms so tight. Please tell me you will remember. No matter how much I do wrong. That I had the best of intentions all along." His smile grew the entire time. That's where she leaned in for their first kiss. She was the only person that mattered in the room that night. That was his mind set.

"I thought you didn't like country?" she asked.

"I don't. I didn't. So what's that tell you?" he said. He smirked again while they continued to slow dance the night away.

He stopped thinking about that dance while he sat on his couch alone. The song was almost through; it only had one more part left, which would actually mean something to him. He held the picture in his right hand while his tears formed one at a time. The room had its shades of light. Every other breath, light from outside would travel in through the window. Light would shine on the couch for maybe two seconds.

"So here I am asking forgiveness and praying that you'll understand. Don't think I take you for granted. Girl, I know just how lucky I am. I know you deserve so much better." He stopped. He let the song conclude on its own.

Time went by as time always does. Every day was a different story. There was always something around that reminded him of his time with her. A song, a picture, a gift, and every time he wanted to extract these certain things. He got rid of everything she ever gave him one day. He put it all in a trash bag. He didn't throw it away though. He didn't have the strength to throw it outside. After the bag sat there for three days, his mother took it outside.

He didn't leave the house; he didn't eat, drink, or anything for that matter. He would sit in the study room, usually reading a book. It was his escape. He would read for hours, basically all day. He wouldn't do anything else. He felt life coming to an end for him. No matter what he did or didn't do, he knew it wouldn't matter because death would come for him in one large attempt. He didn't want to go out and do something big or extraordinary either. That was never his nature.

Some days his mother would come around. She would surprise him by asking him certain questions. One in general would be, "Where's Casey?" After those momentary lapses, she would go back to normal. He would always criticize her whenever she went back to her normal self. One day he even said that she wasn't a good mother. He would regret it days later, although he didn't apologize to her. Even if he did, his mother wouldn't understand in his opinion.

"Life's funny right...ha...I mean, you say things you don't mean, or you do, but it was wrong to say it...and then you never apologize."

"So the change didn't help you at all?"

"It made it harder...I missed her. I knew what was coming."

"What was coming?"

Carter took these long drawn out breaths before getting up from his chair. He pointed towards the restroom. He proceeded out of the room towards the restroom again after excusing himself from the room. It was his routine now. It always consisted of him washing his hands and face. Then he would look at himself in the mirror, always thinking of something.

The football field was back in great shape. It was the intramural field at the local college. It was time to have fun. This was the place for it. He was going to help a friend out today. He would join his team; however, he didn't play quarterback today. He would be at receiver, which was fine with him. He was just looking for good exercise and to have some fun.

He wore his usual outfit, shorts and a white long-sleeved shirt, along with his Giants shirt over the top. Today he even wore a wristband on his wrist, which was a first for him. His hat wasn't around. His black hair stretched over his ears now, as it was getting longer by the minute. He played both ways, playing receiver and then cornerback. He wasn't doing very well at either, although he was having fun.

The weather was okay until the game hit the halfway point. Then slight drizzle appeared; however, the rain would pick up after each minute. Everyone was fine with it though; therefore, everyone kept playing. It was flag football, nothing serious. He ran with the football after a catch; however, after breaking through two defenders, he slipped. He fell in the encasing mud. The drizzle didn't stop while he collected himself on the wet grassy field.

Everyone would dive for passes so they could slide on the ground, as if they were kids again playing back home. His clothes were muddy; however, his face was clean, for now. He ran deep on one play. He had his man burned. The quarterback threw a perfect pass to him and it flew right over his shoulder. He placed his hands out for the catch although the outcome was inevitable. He dropped the pass while everyone yelled in frustration or gratitude. The rain kept coming, harder than a drizzle.

"Nice hands, butterfingers."

"Ha. What are you doing out here?"

"Saw you were playing," she replied. Her entire outfit was clear of rain while he consisted of mud. She stood on the sidewalk with an umbrella perched over her head.

"You know that's dangerous? Walking around, holding an umbrella when it's raining?"

"So is playing football in the rain."

"Did you get the job?" he asked seconds later as he wiped countless raindrops from his eyes. He ran his fingers through his hair, which was completely soaked. She smiled after the question and said, "I did."

"Congratulations."

"Thank you. Now are you coming underneath? Or do you enjoy being rained on?"

He moved off the field without any hesitation. He stood underneath her umbrella while she took off walking faster than he was prepared for. He kept up though, after adjusting to her pace. She took him over to the local coffee shop where there was cover. "So…Friday night, right?" she asked.

"Yeah. You and your father."

He turned off the water. His fear was noticeable in his eyes; however, he shook that feeling after rubbing his eyes again. He splashed the unfailing water on his face. He walked back into the doctor's office two minutes later, although this time the doctor was waiting, compared to the other times. He sat down in his chair.

"Death was coming. Death is coming."

There was a moment of silence after his comment about death. During that moment, it looked as if the doctor was trying to think of something to say; however, he couldn't find a way to put it in the proper wording. Carter noticed. "Doc," Carter said with his famous laugh. Everyone who knew him for more than an hour knew that laugh. The doctor waited for him to say something. Carter was fighting to say it.

"I'm afraid."

CHAPTER 6

▼

HINDSIGHT

"Nothing takes the taste out of peanut butter quite like unrequited love."

—Charlie Brown

It was a Friday night, cooler than most nights, although it still wasn't cold enough for a sweater. He was nervous, for the first time. Every other event he met with her wasn't quite compared to this. For some reason, he changed clothes more times for this event than his clothes for the entire week. He didn't know if he should dress nice, suit and tie, because of the event. It was only a first date, so what clothes would be entitled? It was the little things that he worried about, like what to bring, if he was entitled to bring anything.

He was in a suit, black slacks, black shoes, white long-sleeved button-down shirt with a blue tie, and a blue vest. He did get a haircut this morning; therefore, his hair wasn't as shaggy. It was a formal event, this art museum; therefore, he would be appropriate. He didn't even know anything about art…how ironic.

He looked at himself in the mirror for some reason; he had this system of approval now. He never looked in the mirror before this day. He adjusted his tie while smiling; he approved. He left with plenty of time to do something. That something was important to him. He didn't say a word to his mother as he took a taxi down to a local flower shop. He bought an elegant red rose. He would have bought her a bouquet; however, the occasion really wasn't appropriate for that. Besides, he didn't have any extra money, so she would have to settle for a rose. She would also get one of his charismatic and charming lines. He ended up buying another rose before leaving. He put it inside his jacket. It would be a surprise for later.

He waited outside as he watched others go in, all in tuxedos and better suits than his. His wasn't bad. It wasn't as classy as her father's either, because he saw her approaching. She wore a black dress. It was as if he was shot with an arrow from an angel, because his stare was goofy, at first.

"Wow. You look…incredible." He was going to say something else; however, his attention moved towards her father. His stern look matched his gray hair, which was cut quite short. His beard was brown with slight shades of gray. The father extended his hand and shook Carter's hand. Casey watched Carter's expression because she wanted to see how he would react.

"The rose," the father implied.

"Oh, yeah…it's for you," Carter replied with his sarcastic laugh. Even Casey found it cute. He extended it over to the father as his stern smirk went to an embarrassed look. It happened in front of many people. "I would have gotten you more, but I got caught sneaking through someone else's garden."

"I'm sure," the father replied.

"See? We're getting along already," Casey replied. Carter opened the door for her and let her inside while the father reluctantly followed. Carter circled his head before closing the door behind him. He took a deep breath while loosening his tie; however, he noticed he was dragging behind. He quickly followed while continuing to breath nervously.

The museum was filled with priceless art. That actually explained how Carter felt about art. It was priceless; however, he tried to act sophisticated like other couples. He watched while these older folks studied the painting at all angles. They would talk about its meaning, its "literature," so to speak. Carter would refrain from laughing.

There was a painting she stopped at and her father would mention something eloquent; however, Carter wouldn't be paying attention to the painting. His attention was on Mr. Davis's daughter. He would play it off anytime the father glanced his way. He would look up at the painting, imitating some of the other people from earlier. He held his right hand at his chin while closing one eye. He reopened his eyes seconds later. He would also hold back his childlike laugh.

"What do you think? Uh…"

"Carter, Dad."

"Carter. What do you think?"

Carter copied them from earlier while he looked at the painting from side to side. He rubbed his chin numerous times like her father did earlier. Her father would act quite interested because he thought Carter was being sincere. Casey noticed what he was doing; however, she played along. She thought it was quite funny; however, she held back her laugh as well.

"It's extraordinary."

"That's it," Mr. Davis replied. That's all Carter was going to say. Carter laughed and looked over it once again. He heard someone behind him; therefore, he listened in.

"You know, I actually think that the artist was going for some sort of freelance thing."

She cracked a smile while keeping it hidden from her father. Her father looked at Carter after watching the people behind him, who talked about another painting. He looked the painting over again while Carter pretended to act interested; however, he kept looking over at Casey. She was terribly blushing away from her father.

"I can see what you mean," Mr. Davis replied. He walked over to the next painting and asked, "What do you think about this one?"

"The same thing," Carter replied without even looking at the painting. "What about this one?" Carter walked over next to the father while he pointed at the painting. She followed, and Carter let her walk ahead. Her low cut dress showed her elegant shoulders.

"Now, see this painting? It's just a blob."

"A blob?"

"Yeah. It's not very good," Carter replied. Casey touched his shoulder while leaning up to his ear. She whispered, "I think you should stop while you're ahead." Her father walked over to the next painting and basically pushed another couple out of the way. "What about this one?"

"What did you tell your father?" Carter whispered into her ear as they walked over towards the next painting.

"I told him you were an expert with art." Carter laughed but kept it low. He engaged upon the next painting where her father waited.

"Great," Carter sarcastically whispered. She tapped his shoulder in accomplishment as he went by.

"By the way, you look nice," she said as he passed. He continually chased after her father while bringing up his left hand without looking back.

"Thanks."

An hour later, her father left because he had to go to work. During the entire hour, Carter was taken around the entire museum. He had to make up something every time. He was caught by some of the professionals there; he managed to hide it from her father. He stood in the corner of the room with his head down, chuckling the entire time, while she looked for him. She walked over to him while he looked up from the corner and his smile was huge.

"Now, that was interesting."

"I'm sorry for that. I didn't think he would take much interest, but he likes you. He usually doesn't like anyone."

She grabbed his arm and moved him away from the corner. She put her arm inside of his as they walked around the room. They even stayed for the presentation; he didn't really pay any attention. His attention shifted on her.

"You want to go outside?" she asked.

"Sure."

The night air captivated them as it surrounded the streets. Everyone had their car brought up by the chauffeur, while they stood outside on the steps of the building. "I can't believe you gave my father a rose," she replied with a laugh as they stood outside. She wasn't ready to leave quite yet, so they started to take a walk. During this time, he pulled the second rose from his pocket, which was inside his jacket.

"Well, I'm just full of surprises."

She took the rose. She couldn't help but smile as they made their way around the corner of the building. The wind blew her hair slightly back, and he let her pass first because of a pothole in the road. They walked across the street; he took off his jacket and placed it around her shoulders while the wind started to pick up.

"I didn't actually think you would show up in a suit and tie. I forgot to tell you it was a formal event. I was hoping you wouldn't be embarrassed if you showed up in pants or something."

"It wasn't my first formal thing. Okay, well, it was, but I knew how you would want me to dress for the occasion. It's not the same as playing football in the rain," he replied while they walked around another corner.

They only walked for another ten minutes; however, that brisk walk was just another significant aspect. It would only be the beginning of something great. During those ten minutes, they talked about many different things; however, nothing of great importance. It would be about funny times with family or embarrassing moments, how he was going to substitute for his friend again just so he could play against her.

The moon was radiant as ever, just like her face. Every cloud in the sky shifted around the moon while leaving it untouched. The stars broke with brightness as they walked down the last stretch of sidewalk. Only one streetlight was on, so the light wasn't a factor for seeing the stars.

"I love watching the stars. They're so bright. Usually you can't watch them though, because of all the city lights."

"I know a good spot," Carter replied.

"I'm sure you do."

They stopped at the streetlight while he whistled for a taxi. A taxi came their way as they both looked at each other waiting for one of them to say something. Then they both spoke simultaneously. "Go ahead," he said.

"It wasn't a bad night."

"What were you expecting?"

"I don't know."

"A horrible time," Carter replied. He opened the taxi door while she got in still wearing his jacket. He closed the door although the window was down and she looked up at him. "Have a good night," he expressed. She smiled and replied the same.

"Wait. I have your jacket."

"Hold on to it. It sets up another meeting," Carter replied. Seconds later the taxi drove away. He stood there for a while and kicked a few rocks down the street. He yelled out for a taxi; however, it didn't stop. He yelled out for another one. Again it didn't stop. He took a deep breath. "Crap."

After a taxi finally took him home, he walked the shore for about twenty minutes. He let the breeze hit his tormented suit. He loosened the tie all the way down and stood there for minutes with his eyes closed. The breeze brought spits of ocean water. It wrestled against his face while he imitated what he always wanted to do.

For some reason, he grew to like the clothes. He wore them as he walked down the restless shores, watching the waves captivate themselves one by one. Those tiny rocks withstood the reckoning of the waves. He finally made it to his room after spending countless minutes counting stars. He was tired, although he couldn't sleep. He spent time with his mother up on the lighthouse. He watched with her while she would point out boats every now and then. She would ask him questions about the boats.

"How far out do you think they are?"

"Is that what your father is doing?"

Each time, he would reply the same way, while he held his mother. The window was open so her hair would blow into his face. "Yeah, Mom. They're out there. They're way out there."

He went to sleep after spending an hour with his mother going through the same routine of questions. In the morning, he went back to his usual wardrobe. It was a pair of basketball shorts, Giants shirt, and a Giants jersey. He was going to play in another game. It would be the last for him because next week his friend would come back from his vacation. He would take his spot back.

He sat down at his usual seat in the local coffee shop, reading his sports section after disregarding the rest of the paper. He finished his coffee and finally finished reading the last page of the sports page. She walked in the coffee shop wearing a pair of football shorts along with a Jets shirt. She didn't even go for the counter when entering because her intention was on something else.

"Hey."

"Hey," he replied as he placed his sports page off to the side neatly this time. He looked her over while smirking at the Jets shirt. She sat down across from him at the table, wearing a white cap. Her hair was tucked back into a ponytail. He liked the look.

"Please don't tell me I'm playing you again?"

"You're playing me again," she replied.

"Okay. But I'm not taking it easy on you," he said as he got up from the table. He picked up his paper and coffee before tossing them into the trash can. She followed him outside while they walked across the street, towards the open field.

"Why aren't you going to take it easy on me? I am a girl," she replied. She sarcastically smiled while she held his hand. They walked onto the field. They separated and went to their different teams. She walked backwards while looking at him as he replied. "You're a Jets fan."

"Oh."

While playing, his team was lousy. Before he knew it, his team was down two touchdowns. She started to talk trash as if it was a real championship game. Every time he went out for a route she would hold him and then talk trash to him afterwards whenever he dropped a pass. She would call him "butterfingers," while he went back to the huddle. He would always reply with some comment. "Just wait. I'm letting you feel good."

After ten more minutes, four touchdowns was the comeback role. She kept talking to him, messing with his head while he kept dropping passes. Her whole team started talking trash because his team was undefeated. The game was halfway over. Four touchdowns was the deficit.

"You should have let Carter play quarterback," she said while talking her trash to one of his teammates; however, that's where she messed up. The very next play, Carter came out playing quarterback. She lined up right in front of him. He picked up the ball; everyone was stunned, her included. "What are you doing?"

"You said you wanted me to play quarterback, right?"

"I did not," she replied while blushing. "That was a mistake." He laughed and they continued on with the game. The game changed dramatically, and, when it was over, a team was still undefeated. That day ended with her asking him out to a local dance at the college. Of course he accepted. He found out later that it was a costume ball. He wanted to tell her; however, he couldn't get a hold of her.

Carter finished drinking the water on the desk. He placed the glass back down on its permanent glass mark on the table. He wiped his mouth as he looked around the room, while the doctor entered. This time the doctor went to the bathroom. Carter rested on his favorite chair. He circled his neck before getting up. He started to stretch his tense bones again. He walked over to the bookshelf and looked at one of the books the doctor was actually reading. He knew because he saw a bookmark.

He pulled the book from the second shelf. He opened the book while extracting the bookmark. It was a picture. It was the same picture from his desk, and it was placed ever so neatly in his book. The doctor noticed him with the book; it was in Carter's safekeeping hands. He watched as Carter placed the bookmark back in the book.

"I do the same thing," Carter replied.

"Excuse me."

"You clear out everything, except you can't clear out everything. You leave…something behind, in which…you will remember all the times. I guess that was my mistake," Carter said as he walked over to the doctor's desk. He placed down the five wallet-sized pictures of him and Casey.

He put it right next to the picture frame as the doctor walked behind his desk and sat down. "Why do we keep pictures?"

"To remember," the doctor replied.

Carter picked the picture frame up from the desk and then put it back down a breath later. Carter replied, "To remind us of what we once had…what we could have had…what we will never have again…but of course, there's always the family pictures. Ha…I don't know how to classify those."

"Why do you mention the pictures?"

Carter sat back down in his chair before taking a deep breath. "I've been having…a lot of memories surfacing lately."

"And you're fighting them?" the doctor asked.

Carter coughed painfully as he tried to take another breath. He brought his arms out and tried to pop his fingers although he couldn't. He stretched his arms out again before rubbing his head, as always, with his right hand. "I was."

Popcorn kernels rested on the floor and in between couch cushions while her twenty-inch color television had four sets of eyes focused on the screen. The game was getting underway. There was only one game for them. That would be the Giants versus the Jets. They placed bets minutes before the game; therefore, the stakes made the game even more important. The game was ready for watching.

He sat down on the couch while she dumped the rest of the popcorn on his head. He didn't take notice because Collins was in the middle of a pass; therefore, the bowl of popcorn sat on his head. After the pass was caught, he yelled before taking off the bowl in embarrassment. She would yell in frustration; however, he would kiss her during the huddle, because the commentators kept mentioning great comments about the Jets. He couldn't have her listening to that.

He wore a pair of blue jeans, his new Giants shirt that he bought for this game, and he even had his Giants hat on. She wore a Jets jersey, which she took from her father, although it was cut at the bottom so it would fit her. She wore a pair of tight pants, which Carter couldn't keep his hands off. It was almost half-time. He was still rumbling on about his team…how they were better and how they would win.

They left her apartment at halftime while he took her to a local sports bar. They had been there many times because she watched her Jets games there. The bar was usually for Jets fans; however, he knew it would be split tonight because of the Giants. They arrived there just as the third quarter was getting underway. The bar was crowded with fans, and at every play, everyone would holler in excitement or they would moan in disappointment. She wore her Jets hat while they both sat at a table next to one of the small televisions. She sat in his lap while the Giants scored a touchdown.

Helmets worn, jerseys with stains, and all this was happening while beer circled the room. Everyone had their own set of conversations, laughter, as well as yelling. The Jets scored; she would rub it in while he grew an embarrassed look because of her dance. After a while, she had others joining in on her touchdown dance, even pathetic guys. He would sit there with his hand covering his face in embarrassment.

The Giants would come up with a good play and he would yell along with everyone else. He would engage in high fives with the real fans of New York. "Lucky play. Lucky play," she would say over and over while other Jets fans would agree. After a while, she had her own little section of Jets fans as they started the fourth quarter. He would have his own set of Giants fans. They stood on separate ends, although they both watched each other between plays. He would bring her a drink or a kiss every commercial.

"JETS! JETS! JETS!" she would scream with her newfound friends, while he could only laugh in astonishment. She actually thought that her rooting with everyone else changed the fate of the play. She would send over a note with the next barrage of drinks, and each time it would say double the bet. He would look over at her while nodding his head in approval. He continued to watch the television screen vigorously.

There should have been more nights like that. That was always his thought process. Nights like that are the ones you remember. The game went on as it went into overtime. Everyone at the bar yelled in astonishment while some people started to bet money on the outcome. He walked over to her and held her as they sat down.

"I have a midterm tomorrow," he said.

"I know. Do you want to go?"

"Oh no. We're going to see the Giants pull this one out."

"No way," she replied as she turned her neck to the left so she could look right at him. They stayed that way during overtime, and during a commercial they engaged in a kiss, even with the yelling in the background.

Of course, about five seconds later, the place erupted while beer spilled on his leg; however, he didn't care. He looked up at the television with a huge smile on his face. "What?"

"I told you," he replied as he pointed up at the television. She sighed in disappointment while her cheering sectioned noticed her with a Giants fan. They all started to yell in sarcasm.

"She jinxed us," an insane member of the crowd yelled.

Carter grabbed her as they ran out of the bar as fast as they could. They took the first available taxi, laughing the entire way. "I always knew you were on my side."

"Oh, I was not."

"Right," he replied. He kissed her again while the taxi driver waited for a destination response.

"What was the bet?" the doctor asked.

"She had to go to work wearing a Giants jersey…ha, that was a sight. I have never seen anything so tragic…ha…because she was pissed that entire day. It was kind of like…ha…meeting her mother."

It was a snowy day in Colorado. After skiing earlier in the day, he was surprised by his sunburn. He had to meet her mother today with his sunburn as atrocious as it was. He wasn't even blushing and his face was red. She would tease him; however, he would take it seriously because he was meeting her mother.

He had on at least three sweaters it seemed, an undershirt sweater, with a turtleneck, and then a jacket to cover. He couldn't believe how much apparel he wore. He could barely stand up. He rode an hour in a truck that had no heater. He was cold; she was too, although she got to whine. He didn't; he wanted to sound like a man. The ride was longer than an hour in his opinion because the truck didn't have a radio; therefore, the conversations only consisted of whining about the cold weather, for her, and the meeting the mother, for him. He didn't know what he would say to her. He heard stories from her father about the mother. Of course, you can't always believe stories you hear, can you? They arrived at a beautiful home, which stood three stories tall. It had a white picket fence in the front yard, even though the fence was completely frozen. Icicles formed without any delay.

It was an old colonial home that you only see in rich magazines. He entered inside; it was covered from head to toe with wonderful decorations, paintings, and statues. Her mother walked down from her staircase as she wore a bright pink dress. She had a young man standing next to her; he looked like one of those models you see on the Old Navy commercials, with their flashy smile. Although to Carter, he looked like a Ken doll coming down with a flashy Barbie. This wasn't a moment that Casey was looking forward to.

"Hello. I welcome you to my home," she implied as she shook Carter's hand. She shooed away the Ken doll while her butler came over. "Can you take his belongings up to the guest room?"

"Oh no, don't worry about it. I can do it."

"Oh no, honey. No guest of mine is going to carry his belongings. That's what we have butlers for," she replied as she sarcastically laughed; however, no one else did. She walked away while expecting everyone to follow her as she went to the kitchen.

Her rudeness took its toll after a segment of minutes. Carter wanted to say something, although he didn't because it wasn't his mother. Casey finally said something, although, when she did, her mother ridiculed her. She badmouthed her daughter in front of Carter and he still wanted to speak up; however, it wasn't his place. Casey left the room while her mother tried to pretend as if she didn't say anything wrong. Carter remained in the kitchen with her for a minute at most. He would leave after a question from her.

"Are you and my daughter having sex?"

"Oh God," Carter replied. He exited the room before the mother trapped him with her devastating conversations. He tried to find Casey. It was too big a house. He went from floor to floor, room to room, and then he finally found her hiding on the third floor in the last room.

"Hard to find you in this house."

She was crying on the bed where millions of stuffed animals slept. The curtains were open; therefore, the sun shone in through the window and onto the bed. He walked over to her and sat down on the bed next to her; of course, he had to move and dodge a few stuffed animals. Her face was implanted down on the pillow before her. He ran his fingers through her hair while he brought her face up and into the sunlight. She hugged him and wouldn't let go.

"I hate my mother," she exclaimed. "I'm sorry I brought you up here," she said seconds later, while wiping the tears away from her eyes.

"Don't worry about it. It kind of makes me like your dad a lot more," Carter sarcastically implied. She laughed along with him while he cleared her tears. He gave her a slight kiss to her forehead. "Tell you what. Let's get out of here. We can go stay at the same resort as last time and have a good weekend. Make the most of it."

"I'll start the car," she replied.

Carter leaned up from his seat while coughing again, just like a rerun of television shows. He took another sip of fresh water. The doctor had a smile on his face before asking. "So, the mother was pretty bad? Worst experience?"

"Ha...no...nothing can beat the opera."

After losing a bet on the next game (the Giants lost), he had to go to the opera, again, and it wasn't a pretty sight. He dressed up in the same suit, while she wore the same dress; however, at least she looked great in the dress. She dragged him to the opera. During the entire ride there, he didn't mention anything positive about the opera, while she blurted out everything great about it. Even the driver wanted her to shut up. Carter would laugh at his secretive comments.

They entered the opera house while she stopped to talk to other lovers of the opera. He walked around while trying to find other critics; however, he couldn't find any. He found his seat and he leaned back against the comfortable chair. That's the only thing he liked about the opera. The chairs came perfect for relaxing, even sleeping. Why didn't they just sleep when coming to the opera? It's just like leaving the television or the music on while you go to bed, right?

The talking went on for another fifteen minutes. During that time, he played heads or tails with himself; however, he lost the coin between one of the seats in front of him. He didn't go looking for it. He leaned back against the amazing seat. Before he could fall asleep, she came interrupting.

"Hey. You ready to enjoy?" she asked as she sat down to his left. She held his hand while the audience fell quiet and the stage lit up. "Yeah. Sure. I'm ready," he sarcastically replied.

Three hours of opera, that was what the night entailed. He couldn't deal with three hours of opera, just like she couldn't endure three hours of baseball or soccer. Well, who could? He would rather watch soccer than opera though. He would prefer to be home right now watching his Giants on "Monday Night Football." He tried to sneak his headphones; however, she caught him earlier before they left. She hid them from him.

It was about an hour into the opera when his attention started to fade. His head started to shift away from Casey, and his eyes would close every now and then. Each time, they would stay closed for longer periods of time than before. She kept holding his hand while she grew excited; one of her favorite singers came on stage. She held back from squealing, but then she noticed that Carter wasn't holding her hand anymore. His face was buried back against the seat, and his eyes remained closed. He made slight sounds of snoring, although it couldn't really be considered snoring.

She nudged him; however, he didn't wake. She nudged him again. He opened his eyes while trying to play it off. "I was…just resting my eyes." He moved forward and pretended to be interested in the opera while she looked him over. She looked directly at his guilty eyes.

"You fell asleep," she said as she slapped his forearm.

"I did not," he whispered back.

"You were snoring."

"No, I wasn't," he replied a little louder than the whisper, however. He heard the barrage of whispers behind him. "Shhhh."

"Oh, come on. It's not like you can't hear her singing."

"Carter," she said as she slapped his wrist again. He stopped. He watched the opera with her for another two hours. He almost fell asleep during the last hour; however, she caught him each time he leaned back. He would lean forward quickly as if he were trying to cheat on a test. The teacher kept looking his way; therefore, he wouldn't pull out his cheat sheet. Therefore, he couldn't go to sleep.

She left the opera that night satisfied; she saw the most beautiful play alive. She couldn't have been more content. He left the opera that night satisfied as well, satisfied to be alive after being bored to death. It was nine at night. She wasn't ready to go home yet, and he wasn't either. She couldn't think of anything to do on a night like this, especially with the clothes they wore, until he had an idea.

He surprised her by not telling her where he was taking her. He wanted something uplifting after the opera. He took her to a place where they would have fun. There wouldn't be anyone there to bother them like at the opera. He took her to a place where they could act like kids again, act like the world was one big game. He took her miniature golfing. When arriving, he purchased the hard course; therefore, when they played, they both had trouble making putts.

"This is your idea of a great time?" she asked while she pointed out the tall clown blocking the hole. She laughed at the idea before putting. Her ball was denied again, and she jumped up and down in frustration. He walked up after placing his ball down. She watched, as he wiggled in front of her. He made the putt through the clown for a hole in one.

"Now, that was luck."

"Give me that ball. I'll show you again."

"Oh, you can't do it again," she replied as she handed him the ball. He placed it down on the sloppy turf before putting. It rolled up towards the clown; however, he blocked it with his teeth. It fell right back to Carter's feet again. He kicked the ball up towards the clown; however, the clown denied him again.

"Maybe it was luck."

"Yeah, you only get lucky once," she replied.

"Actually I got lucky twice. Do I get a kiss for luck?"

"No, you get a kiss for a hole in one," she replied as she put her arms around him. A country song played in the background during the duration of their kiss. She started to sway her hips back and forth, to the beat of the music, and she encouraged him to do the same thing.

"No. No, we're not dancing here."

He tried to walk away; however, she followed him, while he sat down on the white rabbit's lap. It was an eight-foot tall statue. She brought him up from his sitting position and she wanted to slow dance with him. "We're dancing. Outside. On a putting green," he said sarcastically. He was going to keep going; however, she kissed him before he could.

They went home early that night, considering they didn't finish their round of golf. It was the first night he spent the night at her apartment. He was late for his midterm the next day, although it was worth it.

"You've had a lot of those lately?"

"What? Memories...dreams of the past. Oh yeah...I have them every night, and sometimes...they seem so real...like I'm back in the past."

"The past can be a good thing."

"What do you dream about, Doc?"

The doctor took his time answering the question, although it appeared as if he wasn't going to answer the question. Carter really wanted to know the answer. "For my son to have a good life."

"I've always wanted to stay in the past...just live there forever...in that moment in time...and try and keep the moment going by living another. I think there will come a time...when I can actually live in that moment again. It'll be home."

Carter got up from his chair as he stretched out again. The doctor already knew what was coming because he did this regularly now. He headed out the door and headed for the restroom. After washing his face again, he looked at himself in the mirror trying hopelessly to focus.

"There's always something that goes wrong in a relationship. Hell, if there wasn't, then what would be the point of having one? I'm not giving you the 'it's over' speech, because it's not. It's not all good times. It's the good and the bad, and that's what makes everything special."

He stopped talking while she collapsed in his arms. Everything that happened in the past few weeks went away. It wasn't a grave mistake. It wasn't something that couldn't be corrected. It was both of them doing something, something other than being together. They both focused on school. They both went out to a party with certain people. It was their first real test. Getting through it was the only thing they wanted to do. Even if that meant him giving a long and tiresome speech, he didn't question it. He knew it had to be done.

Life always throws different pitches at different people. They found out that maybe they weren't ready for a certain pitch; however, all it takes is time. After that certain amount of time went by, it was fine again. It was back to the relationship that sizzled from the beginning. It can't all be loves and kisses now, can it?

Everything changed that day; it had to, for them to move forward with what they wanted. It can always stay in one place, not for her though; therefore, he accepted it. He took it upon himself to show her that he wasn't just in it for the good times. He was going to be there for her either way. He backed it up with more than his speech. He took her to the opera. He even got balcony seats.

During the entire opera, he didn't pay attention to the singing or the yelling in his opinion. He focused on her and how she loved it. He made sure she was taken care of. He wasn't going to let anything come between them again. The problem before didn't matter. There are always problems. Getting past the problem is the hard part.

Carter turned off the water while he looked away from the mirror. He dried his face with an unlimited amount of paper towels. He walked out of the bathroom after looking up at the clock while exiting. He still had plenty of time; therefore, he walked back into the doctor's office.

Again he wasn't there. He noticed his phone was flashing; however, he didn't answer it. He was all for grabbing books off a shelf, although he wasn't going to answer someone's phone. The doctor walked in seconds later and noticed the phone flashing after Carter pointed it out. He pressed a button and the flash was gone.

"Who was it?"

"Nobody," the doctor replied.

"If you have to talk to someone…I could just go…I mean, it's no trouble."

"Believe me, it's no trouble at all," the doctor replied. He slid Carter another glass of water. Carter smiled before taking a momentary sip.

"I have this dream…I'm walking towards my future…and I see a huge bright light in front of me, and…it's calling out my name. The brightness is to my left, and, when I look right…there's Casey. She's waiting for me. I can tell. I want…to go and meet with her…but I can't. Everything in my body and my mind…is telling me to go after Casey, but I'm getting dragged away…pulled…and I can't even say 'goodbye.'"

Carter took another drink from the glass of water before placing it on the coaster. The doctor handed it to him while he was talking. The mark on the table became noticeable now, even from afar.

"What were your dreams? What did you want to be?" the doctor asked. Carter took another sip of water while shrugging his shoulders, as if he didn't know, although he would answer it in a second.

"I wanted to do what everybody does. I wanted…a job or life…that would make me happy. When you're younger…your sights are set on these professions…that are out of your reach…becoming a professional football player…an actor in one of those FBI movies…a music singer…and make millions of dollars. I was like any other kid, except one difference. I wanted to be…Spider-man…ha…I did. I had the comics when I was eight…and that was my dream. It's funny how things change, right?"

"What's your dream now?"

Carter closed his eyes and focused on something out of his reach. "That I changed something…someone out there…some person…a kid…someone.

Changed them for the better. That's about it. I wish I could have been with Casey...get married...raise a family...do all the little things in life that people don't appreciate. Get up at three in the morning to stop your baby from crying...sing him a song...even though you can't sing. It will be those types of things that I will miss...and I don't even have those...ha...how can you miss something you never had?"

The doctor didn't respond; for the first time his attention wasn't shifted on Carter. Carter noticed as the doctor's eyes focused on the picture on his desk. Before Carter could say something, the doctor brought his attention back up and he asked another question.

"Did you ever express any of this to Casey?"

"Ha...no...and I'm sure it would have made her world if I did, because...she was always talking about those sort of things. I never...even mentioned them...even when she brought them up. I was afraid to...because if I did...what would it mean? I didn't know...I thought I had all the time in the world. I thought...that the right time would come...and I could do everything with her...everything she talked and dreamed about. Of course, you can't always...get what you want, but...in this case...it wasn't about what I wanted. It was about what she wanted...and I think that's why I was angry. I couldn't give her what she wanted. Or I was angry because...I couldn't do what she wanted...because I wouldn't be here."

Carter noticed the doctor looking at the picture again. He smiled because he knew what the doctor was thinking of. You could never break anyone from the idea of family. Family is all anyone has sometimes. Carter was going to ask a question; however, the doctor looked up and interrupted him again.

"What do you think of life now?"

Carter didn't answer at first. He was waiting for the doctor to glance down at the picture. He didn't. Carter took a drink of water. He was stalling because he wanted to ask the doctor a question while he looked at the picture. He sighed before answering the doctor's question.

"I think life...life is something...something special. That's all I can say. I can't tell you the meaning...I can't tell you what to do with your life. I can't tell you...what to live for...I can't tell anyone that. What I can tell you...I can tell you...you know what. Why don't you tell me a story?"

"Excuse me?"

"Why don't you tell me a story? Please. Tell me a story about a time you had, and...use that picture to remember."

"I'm sorry, go ahead with what you were saying."

Carter laughed. "No. I really want to hear a story from you. What were you thinking of…right there…right now?"

The doctor laughed but in an embarrassed manner. He slowly worked his way up to telling a story. The doctor looked at the picture again and started to laugh. He looked over at Carter; Carter's eyes rose to a point where the doctor was scaring him because he was laughing at nothing.

"There was a time. I think my son just turned six and he was obsessed with peanut butter and jelly sandwiches. There was one morning when he woke up before us, my wife and I. It must have been five in the morning. He made about twenty peanut butter and jelly sandwiches, and then he brought them into the room. I was sleeping, and so was my wife. He came up with a huge plateful. He wanted to give it to us for breakfast."

The doctor kept laughing while Carter's smile grew. He waited for the doctor to continue. "He woke us up and handed us these messy sandwiches. He spilled them all over our bed, and I still have the stains on the covers. At first we were upset, but he had this look on his face, this innocent look like he messed up. So we each ate a sandwich, and I swear it must have been the worst sandwich in the world. Then my wife smeared one of the sandwiches on my head, and my son thought it was funny, so he did it too. I must have had an entire jar of peanut butter on my face, and I couldn't get my wife, because they both double-teamed me. Sorry, that was kind of a long story."

"It was a good story," Carter replied as he finished his glass of water. He placed it back down on the coaster.

The doctor looked down at his picture before looking up at Carter again. "It wasn't much of a story. It didn't sound like much."

Carter took a deep sigh while getting up from his chair. He walked over to the bookshelf; however, he came right back to the desk. He picked up the picture off the desk, as he looked it over, visualizing the story.

His smile stretched outside the room while he held back his tears from the doctor's story. He placed the picture down on the desk. He paced back and forth three times before walking back to his chair again. He was close to expressing something, although he didn't do it.

"What?" the doctor asked.

"It sounded like a family."

Chapter 7

▼

Never Too Late

"When I despair, I remember that all through history the way of truth and love has always won. There have been tyrants and murderers and for a time they seem invincible but in the end, they always fall-think of it, ALWAYS."

—Mahatma Gandhi

A dream, what does it consist of? His dream was fluent. It always remained the same; he explained it to the doctor earlier. Sometimes dreams told a message, if you believed that. Dreams could tell you something, something you needed to know, or sometimes a dream could just be a dream. He would always think a dream is nothing more than unlimited reality. Could a dream ever change someone's life? That was the question as of right now. Realizing a dream is one thing; however, acting on it is another. Is it too late to go back? Is it too late to do something that you know you should have done a long time ago?

His mind wandered as it always did. A memory would resurface; he would smile from it, because there was never a bad memory anymore. Every memory consisted of her. A dream is different though. A dream isn't real; however, it has every real aspect. So what made it different? His dream would be of him moving towards a new light, towards home, while she waited back in the rules of the earth. He couldn't turn back. He was in a better home, a home at the end of the world, it seemed, and everything he ever knew was left behind. It wasn't really a dream, was it?

It was almost time for dinner, for some people. Night would bring its footsteps closer, inch by inch, but it was still feet away. It was an all-day appointment. He was really taking all day; however, it was something he had to do. The doctor understood that. The wind hurled against the walls from outside. The smell of busy traffic no longer existed in the air. The dream repeated in his mind just like a reoccurring song. He knew he already mentioned it, so why mention it again?

He enjoyed his talk with the doctor so far. He started to realize ideas and the aspect of life while talking about his life out loud. It's always easier to catch your mistakes when reading your writing or saying your thoughts out loud. It's like everything becomes clear for that one moment.

Life would go on after him. He understood that now. He understood that life would always go on, because that's what its purpose was. Hearing about purpose only drove him crazy, although he was getting it now. He started to consider it just like he did when he was a child.

He wasn't in the office anymore. He was doing his usual bathroom break, although, at the point of washing his face, he didn't even look into the mirror. He wasn't going to have another reminder occur. He knew what he left behind. He knew he couldn't go back and correct it. Why go through it again if you didn't have to?

Life changes from day to day, even minute to minute, as well as your emotions and actions. Everything changes, which makes everything confusing. That's the one thing about life which scares people. It scared him. That thought went through his mind every day. Going back and giving in to everything he believed, or was it even what he believed? He didn't know what to believe anymore. He was more confused than ever. Maybe he needed a familiar face to let him know that everything was going to be okay.

Why does life have to be so hard? Some would argue it wasn't. He would feel it wasn't, because he made it hard when it didn't need to be. He made it hard just so he could have an excuse. An excuse was nothing more than a lie. Some would call it a tiny fib; however, a lie is a lie. Even some would argue that.

He walked back into the office with his sleeves down to his wrists. He adjusted his turtleneck and then walked over to the bookshelf again because, once again, the doctor was absent from the room. He looked through the books as he always did. He did this so frequently and often that it seemed as if he came in here every day doing this, although, in actuality, it was only one day. One day can be a life time. One day can take forever to end.

He walked over to his favorite chair in the world. He sat down while relaxing for the millionth time. He closed his eyes as the doctor walked in. He sat down across the table while waiting for Carter to open his eyes. Carter would take his time. He was in no hurry. He finally opened his eyes while wiping his forehead with his right hand. He looked over at the doctor, smiling.

"There's a question you've been meaning to ask me for quite some time now, isn't there?"

"There is," the doctor replied.

"Shoot." Carter smiled as he did in the beginning. He pointed his right hand at the doctor, signaling he was ready.

"What do you want people to remember about you?"

"Wow...that's a good question." Carter took a deep breath before shutting his eyes. He started to talk to himself; however, it was low enough so that the doctor couldn't hear. He wasn't saying anything anyway. It was all mumbling, but. during the mumbling, Carter was actually thinking of an answer.

"I don't know...I was a good person...that I made some kind...of impact. I hope people won't remember me...for this...but for who I was. I just hope they know the real me...and I know those who know me...they do."

The doctor nodded his head the entire time. Carter knew something; however, he hesitated to ask. Finally he decided, the hell with it. "That wasn't the question you wanted to ask? What was the question?"

The doctor agreed and knew he was caught. He pushed his notebook off to the side while looking directly at Carter. "You know the meaning of your dream. Yet you bring it up to me. I can't tell you what to do. I can't tell you to go after her. That's something you have to do on your own. Now, my question is "Why do you want me to tell you to go after her?"

"So you can tell me I'm not crazy," Carter replied.

"Love makes you crazy."

"You know...I should have been nicer to my mom," Carter said as he changed the subject.

The doctor knew what he was trying to do, and seconds later he cut Carter off. "This isn't about your mother anymore, or your father. You know who it's about?"

"I could have done something different...with my mother...I mean, I could have been nicer and helped her. I could...have been there for her...but I wasn't...and maybe...just maybe...things would have been different."

Carter stopped talking while closing his eyes. He started to laugh and then he reopened his eyes. He looked over at the doctor while he had a concerned look on his face. It didn't last long.

"Do me a favor, Doc. Close your eyes…just close your eyes. What do you see? What do you see…when you close them?"

"Nothing."

"Oh…you have to focus…there's something there. There's always something there…believe me. What do you see?"

"I'm back home."

"Is this a dream?" Carter asked while he closed his eyes as well. He put on his red beanie.

"It is a dream."

"Everything you want…is right there…and this isn't about me now. I found my dream…yours is there." Carter got up from his seat as he put his jacket on. He adjusted his turtleneck while he picked up the picture of Casey. He left it next to the picture of the doctor's family. Carter carefully put on his jacket.

"I've learned you need to act on them sometimes…and you helped me with that," Carter said as he started to walk towards the door. The doctor opened his eyes and smiled as Carter looked back.

"Good luck," the doctor said as Carter opened the door. He took one step out before looking back.

"Thanks…you made me realize something. I was given…those few extra month's for a reason." He took carefree breaths while pausing in the doorway. The doctor rose to his feet. He walked over to Carter; however, he stopped a few feet away. Carter pushed the door open in such a pleasant manner.

"Do you need a ride or anything?" the doctor asked.

"Ha. Uh…no…because this is something I have to do on my own. I have to know…if I can do it." Carter walked over to the elevator and rested while he waited. After waiting thirty seconds, he walked into the elevator and he listened to the crappy elevator music for another thirty seconds. He exited the elevator. He took elaborate steps to get outside; when he made it, darkness was waiting. The wind pushed him against the side of the building. He stayed there for numerous minutes trying to catch his breath. He was caught off guard by the outside air.

He was going to seize his dream, capture it, and live in it for as long as possible. "Maybe I should have taken the ride," Carter whispered to himself as he moved away from the wall. He headed down the long, cold, and extensive road.

His mind was telling him things. He was rearranging the words in order so that, when he arrived, he could have the exact wording down. He would repeat it while he walked down the road. He would repeat it like a song. He was trying to learn the words without the music.

"I just wanted to say I love you."

"It has to come from the heart. I've always felt for you…and I love you. No, that was horrible. I need to get this down. I love you, and…there wasn't a day that didn't go by…no. That was horrible to. Damn it!"

He walked across the street while he clung to a car. After making it across the street, he held on to a streetlight for dear life. He couldn't help but laugh the entire time. He did it to overcome his feelings of fright.

"Oh God…if I ever needed you at a time…ha…this is it. I've never asked you for anything…well, lately…ha, and I'm asking for a little help here." He made it around the corner. He was almost to Main Street, where he could find himself transportation. He clung to his jacket as he shifted his turtleneck higher. He kept walking; however, at a pace such that a birthday would have passed by the time he reached the end of the street. He started to whisper to himself yet again: "survival of the fittest."

"Now let's see…I fell in love with you…ever since the first day, and I knew…from that moment on…that you were the one. I messed up…I know, but…I was hoping you would look past that…and take me back. Ha…damn…too dramatic there. Why can't I just say I love you? That will be it right there…I love you. I love you. I love you…I love you."

Main Street was only sporadic minutes away for him. He knew when he arrived he would be ready to see her. He had everything planned out. Everything he wanted to say was in his head right now. He was going over it a second time. "I realized today…I realized I loved you, and I always have…sorry it took me so long…to tell you. Dang, I keep doing it…messing it up. It's not what I wanted to say…why couldn't I just say it…without the entire ordeal. Uh…I love you. I love you…now just say that. I love you."

His body started to shake as his teeth started to chatter. He hated that feeling. He would shiver as if he were trapped in a rainstorm. He would gather himself again after falling against the side of the wall. He stayed against the wall for a more than a few minutes as he tried to keep breathing. He kept saying to himself, "Small steps. Small steps. One step at a time…I have to tell her something first…just that one thing…and that's all I'm asking."

He moved away from the wall while making it around the final corner. Main Street was an eye distance away. He fell to the stoop of an apartment complex. His face was shivering from the cold weather.

"Like I said…I'm not asking for much. At least I don't think…I am. If I am…hell, I'm sorry. Just get me there…that's all I ask…because…I would do it by myself, but…we both know how that goes."

He walked across the street. He waited by a streetlight; however, no transportation came his way. He stood there for minutes and then walked over to a pay phone as he leant up against it. He placed two quarters in.

"I love you…I love you," he said. He hung up the phone and withdrew the change. "I can't say it over the phone. It has to be done in person." He put the fifty cents back in as he dialed another number. He told them he needed a ride. He was on Main Street. He sat down on the bench where he clenched his hands tightly. He kept his mind free for roaming. He would repeat the same thing over and over because he didn't want to lose track of his real reason for going.

"I love you…I love you. Remember when…we went to Colorado, and I…I…dang it. I can't think of the right word to use there. Ha…I will just figure it out when the time comes…oh yeah…ha…that's going to work. Just say I love you…I can't go wrong with…I love you. I love you."

A yellow taxi pulled up five minutes later. It almost took a forklift to raise him from his seat. After rising to his feet, he fell inside the taxicab. He knew exactly what he was going to do; however, he didn't know how he was going to do it. That didn't really matter, did it? He knew he wanted her again. This was the only time he could do it. It was never too late, was it? He would go to her apartment. It would be a journey in itself. It would consist of a taxi, a bus, a train, and then a momentary walk to an apartment complex he had been to many times.

CHAPTER 8

▼

SUNDAY, DAY OF SERVICE, FOOTBALL, AND LIFE

"One word frees us of all the weight and pain of life: that word is love.

—Sophocles

A ten-pound gray cat mannered her way around an occupied couch; her purr wasn't exaggerated. It was louder than a whistling train. She rolled over on his chest while frantically pushing her paws into his side. When he awoke, he ran his fingers over the cat's fur.

He heard it in the background. He always heard it here, the country music coming from her radio. She was in the kitchen cooking breakfast. He would move his head over past the cat, so he could see her. She was in her pink apron. He chuckled because she had a few stains on it already. She always made such a big deal about it. He reached his right hand over towards the table where his glasses were. He put them on while knocking the cat off his chest in the process. He noticed the notebook he gave her on the table as well. He reached for it, brought it up, and he opened it to the fourth page. There was a pen attached to the rings of the notebook; therefore, he snatched it. He started to write on the fourth page after folding the notebook over. He only wrote one paragraph; however, the one paragraph he wrote was the last one. He closed the book after placing it back on the table.

Her back was to him while he got up from the couch. She kept cooking her breakfast. She kept singing along with the country songs as well. He stretched his tired bones before yawning. He walked across the room, while almost hitting the cat in the process. He walked behind her as he placed his hands on her hips. He whispered into her ear.

"You know...you look hideous in this apron." He laughed while she turned around and gave him a deep hug. She wouldn't let go. Her eggs started to burn while she held on to his tired body. She didn't notice even when the eggs started to smoke. "You're burning your kitchen." She turned around and then turned down the heat. She moved the pan away from the stove. She put it into the empty sink.

"There goes breakfast."

"Yeah. You never were a good cook," he replied. He started to laugh again while holding her from behind.

She held both of his hands tighter than ever. "You never complained before."

She escorted him back to the couch as they both sat down, with the cat in between the two of them. He turned on the television and listened to pre-game warm-up for the Giants game. She tried to grab the remote; however, he wouldn't let her get it. She leaned over to get it; he paused and left the remote in her reach. He could only look at her face. He moved her hair from her face while he only had one thought in that moment, "This is what I'm going to miss the most."

She took the remote from him. She turned it on to a church service station. He couldn't stand it. She watched this every Sunday morning. "Sunday is a day of church," she said. He grabbed the remote and changed it back to football. "It's a day of football," he replied. She stole the remote from him faster than he could say his name.

"Okay...okay. We'll compromise here," he said. She nodded her head in agreement as he imitated her while she was thinking. He grabbed the remote again. He changed it back to football.

"Can't believe you fell for that," he stated.

"Oh yeah. Kickoff coming," he said seconds later. She was tired of reaching for the remote because he wouldn't let her get it. She had an idea. She started to tickle his ticklish spot, which was at his ribs. He dropped the remote laughing while she kept doing it. She finally had the remote again. She changed it back to the church service.

The game was on minutes later, because of her. She couldn't watch more than five minutes of the church service either. Even though she hated the Giants, she rooted for them, for this game.

"You hungry?"

"A little," he replied.

"You want to go get something to eat?"

Carter laughed as he turned down the volume for the game. "You want me…to get up, and leave my Giants."

"Yeah."

"Not going to happen," he sarcastically insisted. He turned the volume back up, as she leaned against his shoulder. She closed her eyes while he looked back at the television. However, ten seconds later he turned it off. "Okay. Let's go."

"You sure?"

"Yeah. I need a favor…anyway."

"What favor?"

"I'll tell you later," he replied as she helped him off the couch. He left his jacket resting on the couch. He took off his turtleneck, although he still had on the semi-thick white long-sleeved shirt. He pulled the sleeves up to his wrists as they walked out the door. Of course, she took the lead when they arrived at the stairs. She helped him down one by one.

After the five minutes of moving like the turtle when racing the rabbit, he made it into the car. She drove for home. He looked out the window and looked at all the small shops. He walked by them last night although he couldn't stay long because of the situations.

"You know the favor…I just need to talk with my mother, and…and I might need some help doing it."

He closed his eyes while imaging his home. He imagined the life he had growing up, if it would have been different; however, he realized something. His life was good either way. He looked over at Casey, and smiled. She saw him out of the corner of his eye.

"What?" she said with a girlie giggle.

"You're beautiful."

The sea smell appeared while the sand extended out towards the road. The water didn't reach the rocks today. She drove a 2000 convertible, although she hated having the top down. It was a gift from her rich mother. It was red just like the dress Casey wore to the costume ball. The lighthouse was in eye distance. About two miles away, the road split. "Do you remember the favor?" he asked.

"Yes."

"Change it."

"What?" she replied.

He closed his eyes as he felt the hot sun. He reached for the switch, for the top to come down. Even though she didn't want it to, he flipped it. The top came down, while she coasted at a good ten miles an hour. He pointed out the dirt road that led to the lighthouse. It was near the sand and the shore. She smirked in agreement while driving down the dirt path. It led out to the sand.

"I've always wanted to do this…just never did. I always imitated it at night."

He closed his eyes again while resting his head an inch above the top of the car. He extended his arms out as far as he could both ways. He stayed that way while she drove down the shore at forty miles an hour. The rough breeze hit his face, as well as water and sand, and the meaning of life was brought back. He leaned his head back while his chin was pointed forward. His smile extended towards the sky.

He was somewhere different, for that entire moment, for that ride. He was somewhere where everything made sense, and he didn't have to question it. He didn't need to find the meaning to it. He realized while doing this that he was somewhere different. He was there alone, and he finally understood.

She brought the car back down to a coasting fifteen miles an hour and then ten. She was parked in front of the lighthouse, with water and sand stains on her car. He still remained where he was, nervously chuckling while he brought his left hand over his face.

He was in a good mood. He didn't need any help getting inside. He would almost dance to get inside. It was actually quite funny to Casey. He walked into the kitchen with Casey while she looked through the fridge for something to eat. "What do you want?" she asked.

"I have a craving for peanut butter."

"Okay," she said laughing, because he sounded like a child, a child going in to see his parents after making peanut butter sandwiches. She gathered the peanut butter. She would also grab treats and drinks as she packed them in a bag. "I'll meet you at the hill." She knew what he had to do first. He had to do it alone. She left the house as she headed towards the hill where they always met, for a walk on the shores of Long Island.

He knew where his mother would be at this time, because she was there all the time. She would be in the living room with all the reminders of her husband. She would probably be reading her book right now. She always read her book. She never placed it down during the course of the afternoon. She read it so many times. He understood why she kept reading it though.

"Hey, Mom," he said while entering the room.

"Hey, honey. I was just reading. You want me to get you something? I can. It's no trouble. By the way, how was the meeting with your friend?" She wouldn't let up on talking, so he had to wait for the right time to interrupt. She got up from her chair after placing her book on the table. She gave her son a kiss on the cheek before running over to the kitchen.

"I don't need anything."

"Oh. sure you do. You need to eat something," she replied seconds later. She looked through the fridge; however, after a couple minutes, she walked back into the living room where Carter sat on the couch. She sat next to him.

"What's wrong? You miss your father, don't you?"

"Ha...no, Mom."

"Well, what's wrong?"

"Thanks, Mom. You've been good to me. Thank you...and you don't have to worry anymore," Carter said as he kissed his mother's cheek. He walked away, although it took him a while because he looked up at all the reminders of his father.

"I'm not worried," she replied. He didn't listen. He was looking at all the fishing equipment.

"I finally understand...I do, Mom...I understand." He left the room in a new state of mind. His mother went back to reading her book. He took an entire half of football it appeared, to get to the top of the hill, although he did it. She waited with a blanket spread out, with four sandwiches already made.

He knelt down next to her as she moved close by. He put his arm around her waist while she leaned down against his shoulder. They watched the water while she handed him a sandwich. He ate it, one small bite at a time. The sun made his eyes squint, and his pale face didn't feel pale anymore.

"We've sat on this hill...so many times, and each time...it's always the same, but always different. I wish...that this hill...would be ours."

"It is," she replied. He dropped his sandwich on the dirt. "You want another?"

"Ha...no...it's okay."

"Please tell me you didn't drop it on purpose. I didn't know I made bad sandwiches too," she replied. She started to laugh while he took a bite from her sandwich. It took him forever to chew because she loaded it with peanut butter.

The sun shifted behind a cloud as the wind picked up. It blew right past their blanket and he could feel it. "It's funny...ha...how everything you've ever wanted...everything...is right here...right now...on this blanket. No wonder why I got rid of that sandwich...ha...just kidding. I love you."

The doctor, Doctor Martin, entered his empty apartment, dropped his keys next to the phone before picking it up. He dialed a number that was once his number. He was unsure at first; however, before he could change his mind, something happened. "Hey, sport, how are you? That's great. Is Mommy around?" She came over to the phone. It didn't take long. He was smiling and laughing before he knew what hit him. As for Carter, that day with Casey, the day right now, he lived in it forever. It was better than life.

CHAPTER 9

▼

RECALLED TO LIFE

"By the way, I always thought it was interesting how the only time we see certain people is at a funeral. It's a shame it has to be that way."

—Carter Graham

Carter passed away a week later, during the third quarter of a Giants game, on Sunday, his favorite day. He had his mother and Casey there by his side. He fell asleep on his favorite couch, in the study, and it was his time. They had a funeral for him. He had some unknown friends show up; however, the only real important people were those who were with him for the ride.

It was a beautiful sunny morning, although the temperature still dropped down into the low forties. It would have been a perfect day to the deceased. Fluorescent flowers occupied all four walls of the small church. Ten pews extended back on both the right and left side of the room. The sunlight shone through open church windows as the pastor rambled on with a prayer.

Casey was the only one crying in the room. It wasn't that big a surprise to those who knew him. The church wasn't even filled to capacity, although the most important person was sitting in the front row. Many people didn't come to the funeral after they found out he was cremated.

Casey got up from her seat. It was time for her to say "goodbye," even though she didn't want to do it. She walked to the front of the church, in her black skirt, which Carter never saw. She stood in front of countless strangers. Her tears fell from her eyes to her pale cheeks. She held a notebook in her hand while she used a tissue to wipe away her tears. "Carter gave me a notebook. I thought I would share something he wrote today. It's actually about this day." She refrained from crying, and finally, for the first time all day, respected strangers held back their cries.

"For those of you who read this, I would just like to say I'm okay. I can only imagine what my funeral would be like,...well, not really. I don't think I ever envisioned what my funeral would be like. I don't think many others do either. I can only hope that the weather is perfect, to my liking. For those of you who do know me, my favorite weather is when the breeze is strong enough to push my hair back. When I was told what I had, I could only think of death and that thought existed in my mind until the very end. I urge you not to think of death. I realized it too late, I guess. I should have been focusing on the important things in life. By the way, I always thought it was interesting how the only time we see certain people is at a funeral. It's a shame it has to be that way. I gotta go now, those of you know why."

Casey held the notebook against her chest while she walked back to her empty pew. Service was dismissed, and those people who only see each other during funerals expressed their gratitude towards one another. They discussed his or her jobs while informing each other that they had a baby on the way or that they moved years ago. Casey left while Carter's mother told everyone energetic stories of her son. Everyone listened with the utmost gratitude, as if they had never heard the story before.

That afternoon, Casey walked up the hill where Carter and she had shared so many illustrious moments. She spread out a warm blanket while the wind blew from the shore. It gently pushed her hair back, away from her tearful face. She had an urn with her. She closed her eyes as she stood on that hill. She opened the urn, and she could only envision where Carter was during that moment of relief.

She walked back to her white blanket as the cool air ran across her face. She couldn't help but smile. Carter's notebook, which he left behind, was left unattended to her left. The sun started to set while the waves converged upon every rock, just like any normal day. She hated this weather; therefore, it was perfect for Carter.

The blanket was spread out; however, it wasn't spread picture perfect. She waited for numerous minutes hoping for someone to join her. It wasn't long before she pulled something from her bag. She withdrew a belonging, Carter's belonging. It was a book Carter read many times. The title didn't matter. It was a book which Carter read repeatedly. He would always read it and compare it to other books. There was always another book just like it; however, it wasn't quite like it. This particular book was opened once again. She started at Chapter 1 as she read. For that moment, that one book was recalled to life. The wind picked up as the notebook to Casey's left blew open. It skipped the first three pages and went straight to the fourth. The wind died down as that fourth page was left open for the world to see. The world stopped on that last paragraph.

"I lived, I loved, I did everything a man could do and should do. Death is a part of life and I understand that now. It's not about what you did or what you leave behind; it's about the love. There wasn't a minute of any day that passed by that I didn't regret something, but that feeling will pass, somewhere, someday. Don't feel sorry for me. I'll be somewhere different. I'll be home. Life goes by."

Carter Graham

0-595-33029-0

Printed in the United States
23721LVS00006B/550-576

9 780595 330294